"What are you doing in *my* bed?" Christina demanded.

"And what have you done with my fiancé?" Trembling, she clutched the sheet to her body.

"*Your* bed?" Robert stared at her in disbelief as he hastily covered himself. "This happens to be my room and my bed. But how did you...?"

"Oh, my God," she muttered in shock. "You were in this bed last night. You were the one— the one—" *The one who made love to me like it was our honeymoon.*

"You took advantage of me," she finally gasped.

"Hold on. You got into *my* bed last night. I just did what any red-blooded male would do, uh, under the circumstances."

Christina shook her head. "This is not real. I couldn't have made love with you. I—I don't even know you!"

A smile played around the corners of his lips. "True, we haven't been formally introduced. But we aren't exactly strangers anymore."

Janice Kaiser was thrilled to be asked to write a Wrong Bed story for Temptation. *Honeymoon with a Stranger* contains all her favorite elements—humor, sensuality, a dynamite hero and a romantic setting. Janice and her writer husband, Ronn, enjoyed researching Hawaii and ended up taking a second honeymoon of their own. Look for this talented author's next Temptation story, *Just Desserts*, coming in October 1996.

Books by Janice Kaiser

HARLEQUIN TEMPTATION
477—WILD LIKE THE WIND
508—STAR
530—NIGHT GAMES
556—THE TEXAN

MIRA BOOKS
PRIVATE SINS
FAIR GAME

HONEYMOON WITH
A STRANGER
Janice Kaiser

Harlequin Books

TORONTO • NEW YORK • LONDON
AMSTERDAM • PARIS • SYDNEY • HAMBURG
STOCKHOLM • ATHENS • TOKYO • MILAN
MADRID • WARSAW • BUDAPEST • AUCKLAND

For the real Linda Klein,
a good friend in fact...and in fiction.

ISBN 0-373-25687-6

HONEYMOON WITH A STRANGER

1

HE ATE ALONE, sitting at a small booth next to the window, watching the rain and sipping his coffee. It was early evening. Traffic was moving slowly. Pedestrians under umbrellas trudged along the crowded sidewalk, dodging one another as they headed for home.

There was something about being in a strange city that always made him a little melancholy, though God knew, he should have been used to it by now. Over the past six months he'd been on the road more than he'd been at home. At times he even forgot where he was. At least he never forgot *who* he was. Countless announcers on countless interview shows had introduced him as bestselling, celebrated historian Robert Williams. And the interview questions were just as predictable as the intros. He'd perfected his answers to the point where his anecdotes sounded—even to himself—too glib, too rehearsed.

Thank God it was finally coming to an end. San Francisco was done. Only Portland and Seattle were left on the schedule. But he had three days to kill before his next gig. The question was, did he get on a plane for Santa Fe to have a few days in his own bed, or would that be more trouble than it was worth?

He finished his coffee and paid for his meal. Then he went to the door, wishing he had an umbrella. It was raining much harder now than when he'd left the studio. He pulled his trench coat tight against his body.

Pulling his collar up, he stepped out onto the sidewalk and headed up Post Street, toward his hotel. As he threaded his way through the crowd, he held his collar closed at the throat, but his hair and face were soon soaking wet anyway. He started looking around for a place to duck out of the rain.

Ahead was a bus stop. A small crowd waited under an awning of a shop. When a bus pulled up, the waiting passengers crowded on board and Robert stepped under the awning for a brief respite from the rain. It was coming down so hard that the pounding on the sidewalk was as loud as the roar of traffic. Maybe he *should* go home. At least the snow would be a change of pace.

Miserable, he turned and glanced at the window behind him. The display featured a model of a cruise ship and several travel posters. One caught his eye. It featured an attractive blonde on a sunny beach. She was wearing a hot pink sarong and a lei. The word *Hawaii* was emblazoned over the top of the poster. A sweet pain of remembrance shot through him.

It wasn't that the girl looked like his wife—though Laura had been a blonde, too. What struck him was that she had bought a pink sarong on their first day on Maui and she'd worn it with an orchid lei to dinner that night.

Robert sighed. Their Hawaiian honeymoon had been wonderful, a bit of paradise. The days had been warm and sunny. The nights romantic and balmy. Maui had been as different from a cold rainy day in San Francisco as you could get. What he wouldn't give to be back there right now!

Stepping past the display of posters to better see inside the shop, Robert saw a woman of late middle age seated at a desk. She was talking on the phone. On an impulse, he decided to step inside. When the door opened, the woman glanced up at him, gave him a perfunctory smile and continued her conversation.

Robert began browsing through the rack of travel brochures near the door, happening across one of the Coral Reef Resort and Hotel on Maui. Another clutch of emotion grabbed him. That was where he and Laura had stayed! He studied the photo of a white sandy beach and recalled how they had held hands as they strolled down to the Pacific each evening after dinner to watch the sunset.

"May I help you, sir?" came the voice behind him.

He turned. The travel agent had slipped off her glasses and was toying with them. She absently pushed back a strand of salt-and-pepper hair, appearing a little tired. It was the end of her day.

"I saw the poster of Hawaii in the window," he explained. "It looked inviting."

"Especially on a night like this."

"Yeah, especially on a night like this."

"We've got some wonderful packages available," she said. "Did you have anything in particular in mind?"

He tapped the brochure against his hand. "I was looking at the Coral Reef."

"It's wonderful. Great setting. The golf course is magnificent. Scuba diving, sailing . . ."

"Yeah, I've been there," he said.

"Then you know." She gave him a weary smile, glancing at the clock.

"What's the chance of getting me in for two or three nights?"

She brightened at the question. "When would you like to go, sir?"

"How about tomorrow?"

She laughed. "A day's notice at the Coral Reef in the middle of high season?"

"I'm a gambler."

"More like a dreamer. But let me check. Sit down and make yourself comfortable."

She picked up the phone. Robert slipped off his trench coat, folded the wet side in and sat on the visitor's chair. As she talked, he absently studied the brochure, not even sure why he was doing this. He normally wasn't impulsive.

Several moments later the travel agent covered the mouthpiece of the phone, looking at him. "Miracle of miracles. I can get you a bungalow on the beach. Three nights. They've had a last-minute cancellation."

"I'll need transportation."

She rolled her eyes, then told the reservation clerk to hold the room, pending airline reservations. Five minutes later, it was all arranged. Three nights on Maui, and airfare. Confirmed reservations. Robert handed over his credit card.

"With your luck, I should be sending you to Las Vegas," the travel agent said.

"I'm not even sure why I'm going," he said.

"I'd say the rain out there is reason enough."

Robert absently tapped the edge of the brochure against his hand, then slipped it into his inside coat pocket. "I suppose so."

She took care of the formalities with the credit card, wrote the ticket and gave him an itinerary. Robert thanked her.

"It's a pleasure doing business with you, Mr. Williams."

He unfolded his trench coat and slipped it on. She studied him, her expression quizzical.

"Forgive me for asking a personal question," she said, "but it's been bothering me since you walked in. Why is your face so familiar? And your name, too. I was hoping to figure it out, but I can't put my finger on it. Are you an entertainer?"

Robert smiled. "In a manner of speaking. I've done some work for PBS. I did a history of the Wild West series several months ago and I'm working on a follow-up project for them now."

"That's it!" she said, shaking her finger at him. "My sister loved that program. For several weeks that's all she talked about. Wait till I tell her!"

"Some people have enjoyed it," he said modestly.

"It's really gauche of me to ask, I know," she said, "but could you sign an autograph for my sister? She's been nuts over cowboys and Western things since she was a kid. She has Henry Fonda's and John Wayne's autographs."

Robert took the pad and pen she offered him. "I'm a historian and a writer, not an actor," he said.

"Judy loved your program, though. She'll be thrilled."

He put the pad on the desk to write, leaning over. "Your sister's name is Judy?"

"Yes. Just make it to her, if you will."

He wrote, To Judy, Best Wishes, and signed it, Robert Williams.

"She has your book," the travel agent said. "I'm sure she'll put this inside."

Robert thanked her again, went to the door and stepped outside. The rain had let up some. As he glanced one last time at the poster of the blonde in the sarong, he told himself that he was probably being a damn fool to give in to nostalgia like this. On the other hand, he didn't have anything better to do with the next three days. And when memories of Laura came to mind, as they surely would, he'd just have to focus on the happy ones.

Hawaii had been heaven on earth for him once—a trip to paradise with the woman he loved. And even if the gods didn't see fit to let lightning strike twice in the same spot, he'd at least have a few days of good weather to show for his effort. That had to be worth something.

CHRISTINA CAVANAUGH looked at her watch and sighed. They'd never make it. Bill had been late picking her up. Again. As long as she'd known him, he'd tried to do too much in too little time. That was his nature. Still, she couldn't help resenting the fact that he'd gone to the office to take care of some last-minute business today—when they were supposed to be leaving on their honeymoon. But she didn't complain. What was the point in getting their trip off to a bad start?

To make matters worse, it was raining—a real first-class Seattle downpour. Traffic was snarled for miles. Their plane would leave in twenty minutes whether they were on board or not, and they hadn't even parked.

"We're never going to make it," she lamented as they raced toward the terminal building. "We might as well forget it."

"No way. I'll save some time if I don't park the car. We'll just have to leave it out front."

"But they'll tow it, Bill. That will cost a fortune."

"Sweetheart, this trip is paid for. We're not going to miss it, I promise. We may only make it with thirty seconds to spare, but we're going to make our flight."

Bill brought his Mercedes to a stop right in front of their airline. They both jumped out. He ran around to the trunk and started getting the luggage as Christina ran inside the terminal to check in. There was a long line at the counter. She moaned, knowing that their only chance would be if she forced her way to the head of the line. She felt guilty about doing that when the other passengers had been waiting, but she had no choice. It was either be rude and push ahead in the line, or miss their flight.

Just as she finished checking in, Bill and a porter arrived with the bags. The ticket agent promised to advise the passenger agent at the gate that they were on their way, and she and Bill started running down the concourse.

Bill was puffing as he ran. She'd often chided him for not exercising. Even when she offered to jog at a snail's pace, he wouldn't go with her. Maybe this would be a lesson for him.

Halfway to the gate, he had to stop. His chest was heaving. "I'd say . . . go on ahead," he gasped, "but the plane . . . might leave . . . without me. That'd be a hell of a honeymoon."

"Forgive me for saying so," she said, "but it'd serve you right. Going on a honeymoon *before* the wedding is the dumbest idea you've come up with yet. I'm sorry I let you talk me into it."

"It seemed silly . . . not to go. We'd already scheduled . . . vacation time."

"Yes, that's *one* way to look at it," she said.

Bill caught his breath. He took her arm. "Come on, sweetheart, we're going to make this flight."

They ran, arriving just as the passenger agent was closing the door to the jetway. Bill looked about ready to expire. He was six-three, a large man, though not fat. Soft was the way she would describe him. It bothered her that he neglected his health because she believed in getting exercise and eating right. "If I had your looks, I'd be like that, too," Bill had claimed when she had argued that he should take better care of himself. "You're a national treasure, Chris."

Christina Cavanaugh had been drop-dead beautiful from the time she was fourteen, when she'd begun modeling. She'd been a freshman in high school, with a face that could make millions—if she had enough heart to go for it, as her agent liked to say.

And though she'd liked modeling as well as any job she might have gotten as a student, being a photographer's model wasn't her passion. True, the money had put her through college. But she'd yearned for a career on the other side of the camera—as a TV producer and a writer. Her first job out of college was with the PBS station in Seattle. She'd been there for over eight years now, steadily moving up the ladder, and she loved her work.

Every few months she'd get a call from a photographer she'd worked with in the past, asking if she was available. "Mature beauty is in," one had recently claimed. But she always turned them down.

Christina led the way down the jetway as Bill staggered along behind. The flight attendant in first class greeted them as she helped them to their seats.

Bill plopped into the aisle seat with a heavy thud. He was breathing hard. His brow was beaded with perspiration. Chris sat down next to him, buckled her seat belt and helped him with his. Bill rolled his head toward her, looking like a fox at the end of a fox hunt. She gave him a less than pleased look.

"So I was wrong," he said. "Fifteen seconds to spare—not thirty."

"I suppose I should just accept the fact that this is the way you are," she said, sighing. "You'll never change."

"Sweetheart, have I ever missed anything that's *really* important?"

"We were supposed to be married yesterday," she replied coolly. "And I'd say our wedding ought to qualify as *really* important."

"I know, sweetheart. But I did give you two weeks' advance warning, so it wasn't a last-minute thing. Besides, you know the conditions were completely beyond my control."

Christina tossed her long auburn hair over her shoulder. "Yes, I know. You're still married. I can hardly fault you for not wanting to go to jail for bigamy."

"It's a minor legal complication," Bill protested. "You know that, sweetheart. I was positive Kelly and I would have our financial settlement worked out by now. She's every bit as eager to remarry as I am. In fact, she got engaged first."

"I understand all that," Christina said.

"We'll get married this spring. May at the latest."

"I know, Bill. I'm not blaming you," she said. "But I feel strange going on a honeymoon when we aren't married. It seems . . . I don't know . . . sacrilegious or something. Or maybe it's just embarrassing."

Bill stroked her cheek with the back of his finger. "If it makes you feel better, think of it as a sexy weekend."

Christina sighed. "Yes, that's what I've been telling myself."

"Then what's the problem?"

"Maybe women are less flexible about things like this than men. For four months I've been planning on getting married this weekend and going on a honeymoon in Maui. I romanticized it, I know, but people do that about their weddings. After all, this was supposed to be the first day of a whole life together, as man and wife."

Bill leaned over and kissed her cheek. "Chris, honey, you know I love you. In the end, that's all that matters."

She nodded, feeling guilty for having complained. The last thing she wanted was to act like a spoiled brat. After all, Bill Roberts was the man she wanted to marry. So why let a little glitch like his still being married get in the way of her happiness?

"Don't worry," she said, squeezing his hand. "I'm going to do my best to be cheerful. I promise. All I want is for us to have a wonderful time."

"Believe me, you'll have the time of your life."

He leaned back then, took a deep breath and closed his eyes, apparently satisfied that the issue was settled. But Christina wasn't so sure. No matter how much she wanted to believe him, she had a funny feeling that this pseudohoneymoon of theirs wasn't going to turn out to be the dream trip they'd planned.

2

ROBERT WILLIAMS strolled across the beach, watching
the sun slip toward the horizon. Maui was beautiful.
The balmy tropical air and picturesque seascape evoked
a thousand mental snapshots of Laura. Ten years ago
this month, they'd walked hand in hand along this
beach, terribly happy and deeply in love. A January
honeymoon.

This wasn't his first trip back to the Islands since
then. They'd returned together once, not long after they
found out she was pregnant. They'd stayed in Honolulu for a couple of days so he could do some research
at the university, then they'd flown to the Big Island so
he could check out cattle ranching operations for a
book he was doing on Hawaiian cowboys. Laura hadn't
felt well and had spent most of the time in their hotel.
Two months later she was dead.

The Coral Reef had been remodeled in the interim,
but much remained unchanged. Robert decided he'd
take his walk down memory lane first, to get the pain
of nostalgia behind him. He'd learned over the years
that the best way to meet a problem was head-on. So
he'd spent the afternoon retracing their steps, visiting
the places they'd gone, reliving it all. Then, once it was

out of his system, he'd look forward, try to enjoy the rest of his trip.

He'd flirted with the notion of finding a woman, if only for a drink and conversation. The problem was the Coral Reef was not the sort of place that tended to attract singles. It was a place for couples. Still, it wouldn't hurt to look around.

With dusk falling, he returned to his bungalow for a quick shower. After he'd checked in he'd gone to the hotel shop to buy a pair of white linen slacks, some shorts for daytime, a swimsuit and a few Aloha shirts. One of the shirts was green, a color he liked because it looked good with his sandy hair and green eyes.

Wearing the linen slacks and the green shirt, Robert headed off to the hotel bar. That would be the best place to get the lay of the land.

IT WAS DARK by the time they parked in front of the Coral Reef in their rental car. Christina was positive the gods were making an example of them, though what her sin was, she wasn't entirely certain. Maybe fate was telling her that spinsterhood wasn't a bad life alternative.

"The day from hell," she muttered, as Bill turned off the engine to the car.

He sighed, not seeming pleased. But neither was he willing to contradict her. "Well, at least we made it."

"Barely."

"Cheer up, sweetheart. Our troubles are behind us."

"There's still plenty that can go wrong," Christina said. "We could walk in there and they might never have heard of us."

"No way," Bill replied. "I've got written confirmation of our reservations."

They looked at each other, both exhausted. Christina took his hand. "I'm a firm believer in destiny," she said. "And something tells me our troubles are only beginning."

Bill laughed. "Well, let's see. First we lost three hours when the plane developed engine trouble an hour out of Seattle. Going back for repairs made us miss our connecting flight. Then the airline lost our luggage, and the first rental car they gave us wouldn't start. Of course, the second didn't have any gas in it, so it wasn't much better. But the third was the charm. I'd say our bad luck has pretty well run its course."

"I wish I shared your optimism."

"What else can go wrong?"

"I'll bet you ten bucks they've given our room to somebody else," she said.

He shook his head. "No way. After what I've been through today, I promise you, Chris, if they don't have our room, I'll own this place by sunup."

"I'll start believing you if I ever see my suitcase again."

"They sent our luggage to the Philippines, sweetheart, not hell."

She had to admire Bill for his tenacity and his optimism, if nothing else. Without a thing to wear, she was

ready to get on the next plane for home. But he'd regarded it as a chance to get a new wardrobe. "You can
either look at a glass as half-full or half-empty," he'd
said.

Two attendants in Hawaiian shirts arrived at the car,
each opening a door. "Aloha," they said cheerily.

"Let's hope so," Christina said.

"Where's your luggage?" one attendant asked Bill.

"About halfway to Manila by now. At least, that's
my best guess. We'll be making a stop at the hotel
shop."

The other man helped Christina out, giving her a
sympathetic smile. Fortunately, she had her carry-on
bag with her toiletries and a change of lingerie with her.
But she would need one or two things to wear until their
luggage arrived—assuming it would be found, of
course.

They went inside and she found a comfortable chair
while Bill registered. The Coral Reef was casually elegant. The main building of the resort had a high open-
air lobby that was filled with tropical plants. Christina
looked around, reminding herself that this was her
honeymoon and she should be happy.

Bill was trying . . . and he really did love her. Actually, he was crazy about her, which was a good part of
why she'd agreed to marry him. Bill was an entrepre-
neur who'd started a phenomenally successful chain of
coffeehouses. He was public-spirited, kind and very
active in charitable work. They'd met when he agreed

to underwrite the children's television program she developed over a year ago.

Bill had an effusive, outgoing personality. His cleverness and charm were the primary reasons for his success. On the day they met he'd told her he was in love with her—no ands, ifs or buts about it. Of course, his cause wasn't helped by the fact that he was married, though he was legally separated. Kelly had taken off for California with her lover, leaving Bill to figure out how to dump her without forfeiting half his sizable fortune.

At first Christina was concerned that he was on the rebound, but she soon learned that the marriage had been over for a couple of years for all intents and purposes. The problem when she met him was almost entirely financial. Still, she had proceeded with caution. She liked Bill. He was attentive and devoted. But she wasn't sure for a long time if those feelings justified marriage.

Christina noticed that the registration process was taking an unusually long time. She was seated far enough away that she couldn't be sure what was going on, but it looked like there was trouble. But rather than going to the desk to find out what had happened, she wandered over to the open side of the building that looked out onto the Pacific. It was dark now so she couldn't see much beyond the flaming torches that lit the perimeter of the grounds.

The air was soft and fragrant with the scent of ginger. She stared out, watching couples strolling arm in arm as they crossed the grounds. Soft Hawaiian music was playing in the background. If she listened carefully, she could hear the gentle pounding of the surf. Maui was definitely the kind of place to be with someone you loved.

Christina spotted an older couple sitting on one of the many benches. For some reason, the woman reminded her of her mother. Marlys Cavanaugh had died two years earlier, before Christina had met Bill, and she'd really missed having her around to talk to—especially after Bill proposed and she'd had to decide what she really wanted in a husband.

Christina's father had met a widow on a cruise a year after her mom died, and soon thereafter remarried. Stan Cavanaugh lived in Florida now. Chris spoke to him every month or so, but she'd never felt comfortable discussing her love life with him. They didn't have that kind of relationship.

Still, he'd tried to be supportive when she'd finally told him about her decision to marry. "You're getting older, honey," he'd said, "just like the rest of us, and your Bill sounds like a real nice fellow." Christina took that to mean "well qualified."

She'd tried not to look at their relationship the way her dad did—in practical terms—though at twenty-nine she knew she wasn't a girl any longer. Her romantic notions of passionate love had long since been tempered by a healthy dose of realism. In her early twenties she'd had two intense relationships. She'd seriously considered marrying both times. But something had held her back. After a while she wondered if she wasn't unrealistic about what she wanted.

About the time she met Bill, Christina had begun thinking more in terms of a man's qualifications than the passion he might evoke in her. She did care deeply for Bill. And he was clearly head over heels in love with her. That had to count for something.

Christina was still staring dreamily out at the tropical night, letting her thoughts wander, when Bill slipped up behind, putting his arm around her waist. With his other hand he held a ten-dollar bill in front of her.

"You win," he said sheepishly.

Her mouth dropped open. "You're kidding."

Bill shook his head. "No, our room is not available."

"Not available? Checkout time was hours ago."

"Apparently a pipe burst in the bungalow and they're working frantically to repair it. They aren't sure they can get it ready for tonight."

Christina's shoulders sagged. "Oh, Bill, what are we going to do?"

He tapped the end of her nose with his finger. "Love conquers all."

"Yes, but sleeping on the beach is not my idea of a honeymoon."

"They've made a little room over the boiler or something available on an emergency basis. After we buy some new duds, we can use it to change and get cleaned up. I strongly encouraged the assistant manager to re-double his efforts on the bungalow. I think I persuaded him of the importance of your being able to hear the surf outside the window when you go to sleep."

She put her arms around his neck. "Poor Bill. You've had to threaten people all day long. This trip has to be even more miserable for you than it is for me."

"It was the only way to get what I wanted, unfortunately. When I threatened mayhem, the assistant manager assured me we'd have a room, a decent room, by midnight. Meanwhile, we'll be having an elegant dinner on the house."

They hugged, and Bill kissed her, but Christina couldn't help feeling a deep sadness. She wasn't normally superstitious, but this had to be some sort of omen, no matter what Bill said. It just had to be.

ON HIS WAY TO THE BAR, Robert had decided to linger in the gardens for a while. He was sitting on one of the many benches, enjoying the air, when she suddenly appeared at the open side of the hotel lobby. She was standing next to a pillar, staring out at the night. And she was so beautiful, the sight of her had virtually taken his breath away.

The garden was below the lobby, so his view of her was upward, through the palms. It was difficult to say just what it was about her that dazzled him. Her face was lit by moonlight and her lithe figure was silhouetted by the light coming from within the building.

The way she stood, the way she held herself, added to the allure. Had she been in a filmy gown instead of pants and a tank top, he might have mistaken her for an apparition. But this woman was as real as she was incredible. Incredibly elegant. Incredibly sexy.

Everything about her seemed calculated to entice him—the way she casually lifted her long auburn hair over her shoulder, the way she turned her face toward the moon or canted her head to catch the fragrant night air. Watching her, his mind had leapt at the possibilities. Had this perfect stranger been sent to him by the gods?

He could have stared at her all night, and would have, except that another man came up to her and put his arms around her waist. It was bad enough to discover that she was taken; it was worse to actually see her with another man. When they kissed and walked off, holding hands, Robert felt more empty and bereft than before.

He decided it would have been better if he'd never seen her, except perhaps for the value of the lesson it taught him—that his heart craved more than just sex. He wanted to find love again, love with a woman who could fulfill his unfulfilled self. Love with a woman like the goddess he'd just seen.

And yet, he knew it was foolish to romanticize the woman on the balcony. Beautiful though she was, she could've been stupid or selfish. Her lovely face might well have masked a character without substance and a soul without conscience.

Still, seeing her had given him a renewed appreciation for his ability to feel, and to feel with passion. Sighing, Robert got up and headed off to the bar, wondering how long it would be before another stranger would come along like that and knock him on his heels. These things, after all, did not happen every day. How many such opportunities came along in a lifetime? Two or three, maybe?

At thirty-seven, Robert figured he'd probably only have a few more chances to find the kind of perfect, truly passionate love he craved. He hated to think this might be his last-gasp effort to find a soul mate.

That was a hell of a bleak thought, he decided. One that demanded to be washed down with a nice stiff vodka tonic. Besides, a drink would be a good place to begin his descent back to the society of mortal women—assuming he was fortunate enough to find even one of those. But with his luck, the single glimpse of the goddess with the dark flowing mane would end up being the high point of his evening, if not his trip.

3

"WE GET SOME honeymooners this time of year," the barman said, "but I'd say more older couples escaping winter, married professionals and the usual assortment of guys with mistresses or secretaries, if you know what I mean."

Robert sloshed his drink in his glass. "But not many single women."

"A few. I noticed two or three by the pool this afternoon. Sometimes they come in pairs for a little winter vacation. But if you're looking for action, I'd suggest the bars in Lahaina."

Robert gave the barman, a stocky Hawaiian named Joe, a lazy grin. "I'm not desperate. Just curious."

Joe leaned over the bar and, in a confidential voice, said, "Off the record, there are options I can help you with, if you know what I mean."

Robert smiled and sipped his drink. "Thanks, I'll keep that in mind."

Joe went off to mix drinks for the cocktail waitress and Robert stared out at the night. The bar was open to the garden and filled with so many tropical plants that it was difficult to tell where the inside ended and the outside began. An artificial waterfall behind the horseshoe-shaped bar seemed to spring out of a natural rock formation, adding to the effect.

Robert's thoughts returned to the woman he'd seen earlier. The recollection of her sent an ache of longing through him. He wondered about her relationship with the man. Mistress? Wife? Girlfriend? Or could they be newlyweds? Somehow that seemed the most logical. She didn't seem like the type who'd be some guy's mistress, but of course he had no firm basis for that assessment. He was projecting, idealizing her.

Robert shook his head with self-deprecating bemusement. It was sad to think that the only consequence of having seen such a gorgeous woman was to point out how deficient his life was, how emotionally empty. Not that he was unhappy. He wasn't. But in taking a nostalgic trip back to Hawaii, he'd risked discovering what was missing from his life. And he'd quickly learned that professional success was good, but it certainly wasn't enough.

Robert tried to decide whether to have a second drink or head into the dining room for dinner when he heard a loud crash. Turning, he saw a man sprawled on the floor at the entrance to the bar. A tray of food and a busboy were next to him. The boy scrambled to his feet.

"Sorry, sir. Sorry," the busboy said pleadingly as he took a plate of food off the man's legs.

"What in the hell are you doing running around the corner like that?" the man roared as he sat upright, lifting chunks of fish off his shirt.

Robert decided no one was seriously hurt, so he didn't offer assistance. Other employees were arriving to help with the mess. He was about to turn back when he saw her again—the woman he'd seen from the garden.

She had changed and was now wearing an emerald sarong. Robert heard himself moan as he gazed at her. She was helping the man get up. Once she had him on his feet, she flipped her long auburn hair over her shoulder, using the same gesture he'd noticed earlier. The grace with which she did it sent a tremor through him. She was stunning, breathtaking. Her voice drifted into the bar.

"Bill, are you all right?" he heard her say.

The man was looking at his elbow as restaurant employees dabbed at him with towels. He was red in the face and angry as hell.

"Send somebody over to the men's shop to get another one of these damned shirts," he groused. "And don't put it on my tab!"

He was surrounded by half a dozen staff, including the hostess, a pert Asian woman. "Your dinner will be on us this evening," she was saying.

"It's already on you, damn it! You've flooded my room!"

Robert couldn't help but smile. The poor guy seemed to be having a really bad day. But he didn't watch the man for long. The woman drew his attention. He was spellbound just looking at her.

She was astonishingly beautiful. She had large, wide-set eyes, fabulous bones and a sensuous mouth. Her nose was narrow and straight, her jawline perfectly drawn, suggesting strength, as well as femininity. But it was her thick mane of rich auburn hair that gave her a particularly regal air—that, and the way she held herself.

"Poor darling," she said to the man. "What else can happen to us?"

"God only knows." He shooed away the fussing entourage. "Listen, why don't you have a drink in the bar while I go back to that janitor's closet they gave us and change."

"I'll come with you," she said.

"No, the elevator cable might snap and there's no sense both of us being brutally crushed."

She laughed, running her long, slender hand over his cheek. "Poor thing, you don't deserve this."

He kissed her hand. "It's you I don't deserve, Christina. You've been a saint."

"*Christina*," Robert said under his breath. Now he knew her name. But he still wasn't sure of her relationship with this Bill. They weren't a long-married couple, judging by the way they interacted. He'd guess they were on their honeymoon. The mere thought of that was painful—it denied him his fantasy.

"I'll be pleased if we make it home alive," she said.

"I'm not willing to bet on that at this point," he replied. "But go on in and have a drink. With luck, I'll be back shortly."

She patted his cheek and Bill went off. Robert's breathing stopped when she turned and faced the bar, looking almost directly at him. She didn't appear to see him, though. She just strolled in, taking long, graceful strides. It was as if fate were delivering her to him.

The hostess led her to the far side of the horseshoe. Christina climbed gracefully onto a stool, directly opposite him. If she noticed him at all, there was no special recognition. Robert had the presence of mind not to stare with his mouth hanging open, but he couldn't stop looking at her.

"We're buying for Mrs. Roberts, Joe," the hostess said to the barman. She turned to the guest. "I'm so sorry about what happened. I hope the rest of your evening will be more pleasant."

"It can only get better," Christina said.

The hostess nodded and went off. Christina glanced at Joe and smiled. Robert stared at her lips. He was thinking what it would be like to kiss her when it hit him that the hostess had called her "Mrs. Roberts."

"What can I make for you, ma'am?" Joe asked.

"Is there such a thing as a double Mai Tai?"

He grinned. "I can make you two?"

"That'll work. I'll drink them one at a time."

"Yes, ma'am."

Joe went off to prepare the drinks. Christina looked across the bar, seeing him for the first time. He couldn't say it was recognition, because there was nothing to recognize, but her eyes fixed on him for a moment.

It almost seemed as though she might speak to him, but they were too far apart for conversation. Robert considered making a remark, the sort one could call across a room—"Paradise isn't what it's cracked up to be," or, "Heck of a way to get a free drink"—but he decided not to intrude on her space. Besides, if he talked to her, it might destroy the fantasy.

Christina didn't look at him for long. She turned and stared out the open side of the bar, interlacing her fingers in front of her. Her profile was exquisite. With her auburn hair cascading down her back, he was able to see her long graceful neck. She presented a stunningly elegant image, one of classical beauty, the sort one saw in a sumptuous fashion magazine. He savored her, not as a hunter or a predator, but as a connoisseur of beauty taking pleasure in a fine piece of art.

Joe, the barman, delivered Christina her Mai Tai, for which she rewarded him with a warm smile. She immediately took a long sip through the straw, then sighed.

"Ah. I needed that."

"Your second will be ready when you are," Joe said.

"Thanks."

Joe moved around to Robert's side of the horseshoe, dabbing the hardwood with a bar towel here and there. "How about you, sir? Another vodka tonic?"

"Why not?" Robert said, then added under his breath, "The view here has improved in the last few minutes."

Joe glanced over his shoulder at Christina. "She's a looker, isn't she?"

"If you've got one like her in your bag of tricks, my man, I could fall off the wagon."

"Who wouldn't?"

"The stuff dreams are made of."

Joe glanced toward the entrance to the bar. "Do you suppose her husband appreciates what he's got?"

"He's a fool if he doesn't."

Joe nodded. Then, sighing, he went off to prepare the drink. Robert studied Christina again. She was looking down at her glass, turning it absently, perhaps thinking about the man she loved. For some reason, that made him do something he normally didn't do— he began comparing her to Laura.

His wife had been attractive, though she wasn't the beauty Christina was. There was a soft femininity about them both, and he was willing to bet the similarity didn't end there. He sensed that Christina had Laura's inner strength and intelligence. Some pretty faces were blank. But the lady seated across the bar appeared to him to have substance.

Joe put Robert's drink down in front of him, noticing his attention was still focused on Christina. "Take my advice, man, and head down to Lahaina."

Robert gave him a crooked smile. "But it's so much fun to fantasize."

"So what brings you to Maui all alone?"

"Catching a breather in the middle of an extended business trip. The rain on the mainland was getting to me."

"I can understand that. I spent a couple of years in San Jose, going to college. Thought of staying, but the lure of the Islands was too great. The climate gets in your blood."

"Maui has lots of special memories," Robert said. "Spent my honeymoon here at the Coral Reef."

"No kidding?"

"Yep."

"You divorced?" Joe asked.

"No, a widower. My wife died four and a half years ago."

"Sorry to hear that."

"She died much too young."

"Accident?"

"Ectopic pregnancy. I came home and found her in the bathroom, unconscious. She'd had a massive hemorrhage. Died hours later at the hospital."

Joe shook his head. "That's rough."

"Yeah." Robert watched Christina sip her Mai Tai as a stab of sadness went through him.

"Same thing happened to my sister-in-law, except she made it."

"Laura might have, too, if I'd found her sooner."

"Bummer."

Robert nodded and sipped his drink. Joe drifted off to serve an older couple who'd taken seats at the top of the horseshoe.

Robert imagined what it might have been like if Christina had come to Maui alone. He'd have felt free to approach her, find out what she did for a living. Of course, it was unlikely she had any interest in the Old West, but it was fun to imagine that she did. Hell, even being willing to listen to him ramble on about it would be thrilling.

After Joe had tended to the couple, he made his way over to Christina again. "Ready for another?" he asked.

"No, I think I'll slow down. I've heard these can sneak up on you," Robert heard her say.

"You heard right."

"On the other hand, considering the day I'm having, I might be better off unconscious."

"I've seen a number of people arrive here stressed out from the travel," the barman said. "I've got some good advice."

"At this point I'll listen to anything."

"Before you head off to bed, go down to the spa and have a massage. Believe me, a few drinks and a world-class massage and you'll be a new person. The best way in the world to forget your troubles."

"Thanks for the suggestion," she said, taking another sip of her drink. "I just might do that."

Bill Roberts arrived, sauntered over to the bar and sat next to Christina. "Believe it or not, the sky didn't fall on me."

She laughed. "It didn't fall on me, either."

"Maybe we'll survive long enough to get through dinner."

Two more couples arrived and the din of conversation became loud enough that Robert could no longer make out what Christina was saying. It hardly mattered, though. His fantasy definitely did not include Bill Roberts, and he had no desire to know them as a couple. Still, he gave the woman a last wistful look when she and her husband headed off toward the dining room. Robert silently said goodbye. It had been a pleasant daydream while it lasted.

THEY WERE at the best table in the restaurant, seated on the side of the building facing the ocean. Christina rested her chin in her hand. Her eyes were closed and she was enjoying the balmy air. She inhaled deeply, savoring the rich scent of ginger that permeated the air.

"I've never seen a more beautiful sight," Bill said.

She opened her eyes and saw her beaming fiancé. She smiled back. The room was not quite spinning. "I'm feeling mellow," she said, "I can tell you that much."

"After three Mai Tais, it's no wonder."

"I hardly ever drink this much, as you well know," she replied, "but something about today brought it out in me."

Bill, who'd had a few himself, nodded. "I know just what you mean." He checked his watch. "It's after nine, sweetheart. We still have two hours before the bungalow is ready. They're saying eleven now."

"That's a long time," she said. "There could be a tidal wave, an earthquake, a volcanic eruption or a civil war in the next hour. We might not live to see the inside of that room."

He grinned. "Well, my love, I wouldn't bet against any of those possibilities. Not with our record."

She looked into his milky gray eyes, trying to keep him in focus. "Tell me the truth, Bill. Do you think it's us?"

"Is what us?"

"All this bad luck."

"Of course not. Until this morning things have gone perfectly," he said.

She wasn't so sure about that. In fact, this trip had brought out something that she'd been denying, even to herself—her first real doubts about their relationship. She'd refused to face it till now, but in recent weeks doubt had begun to creep into her heart.

She knew it was unfair to allow a horrible day like this to affect her so strongly, but as the hours had passed, she began realizing that she was glad their wedding plans had gone awry. She wanted to love Bill, and in her way she did, very much. But did she really want to be his wife? Her head said yes, but her heart wasn't so sure. That was a shocking admission, so shocking she was ashamed.

Just thinking such thoughts made Christina feel guilty. Still, maybe it was a good thing Bill's settlement with Kelly had developed complications and their marriage had been put on hold. It gave her the opportunity to use their honeymoon to test her feelings. Better now, before the wedding, than after.

"Why the pensive expression?" Bill asked. "I hope you haven't let this circus get to you."

Christina shook her head. "I guess I'm just tired."

Bill reached across the table and took her hand, squeezing it. She looked down at his fingers, feeling traitorous. She'd allowed herself to get into a funky mood. Maybe the Mai Tais were keeping her from thinking straight. Alcohol usually had a down side, though it did melt inhibitions. But she wouldn't let herself say anything to Bill, not something she might regret in the morning.

"It really bothers you that we had to postpone the wedding, doesn't it?" he said.

"It's not your fault. If anybody's to blame, it's Kelly."

"She thought with our wedding date set she had leverage on me. It was either give away those extra millions, or hang tough."

"I know, Bill. You don't have to justify it. I've told you I understand."

Christina sucked the last of her Mai Tai through her straw. It was sad to think that this honeymoon of theirs actually made her want to get drunk. How could that be anything but a bad sign?

"You know what," Bill said, "I think you ought to go to the spa and have that massage you were talking about."

"No, that's a silly self-indulgence."

"I really think you should. I want you to pamper yourself."

"Why don't you have one, too?" she said. "You could use a massage as much as I could."

"No, I intend to keep after these folks. An hour or so from now that bungalow of ours is going to be ready one way or the other, I promise you. I want to make sure everything's perfect. After all, this is the first night of our honeymoon and it's supposed to be very special." He pulled her hand to his lips and kissed her fingers. "Am I wrong?"

Christina shook her head. "No, Bill, you're right."

"Come on then, sweetheart. I'll walk you down to the spa."

4

ROBERT HADN'T BUDGED from his bar stool. While traveling, he normally avoided bars. A beer or a glass of wine with dinner was all he usually had to drink. But he was rooted to the spot.

Actually, he hadn't had much to drink. The dregs of his second vodka tonic were still in his glass. But he'd sat there, almost as if he were in a trance, thinking about Christina.

Most of the other patrons had gone off to dinner. A few were already back for their nightcaps. If he wanted to eat, he should go now, but he wasn't all that hungry. He could always get something from room service later.

As he pondered the weighty issue of what to do with the rest of his evening, a face across the bar came into focus. It was a woman, a blonde, sitting in practically the spot where Christina had been. She was bosomy and wearing a rather low-cut, provocative white dress. She was also looking right at him. And smiling.

Robert watched her watching him. She sipped her tropical drink without taking her eyes off of him. All indications were that she was on the make. No one else was seated at the bar. Joe, the bartender, had gone into the back for supplies. There was just himself, the blond bombshell, the balmy Maui air and the tinkling water-fall.

"Kind of lonely in here, isn't it?" the woman said. She had a breathy little-girl voice.

"Yeah," Robert replied, "seems to have emptied out."

"Guess that means we can't be strangers looking at each other across a crowded room then, can we?" she quipped.

He chuckled. "I guess not."

She sipped her drink, still looking at him. "You with anyone?"

Robert was mildly surprised by her brazenness. "Only my invisible dog, Spot."

She laughed more heartily than his joke deserved. "It's not very ladylike of me to ask, but mind if I come join you?"

Robert shrugged. "Be my guest."

She got up and carried her drink around the horse-shoe bar. She looked to be in her early thirties. Her brow arched slightly as she slid onto the bar stool next to him.

"Hi, my name's Patsy," she said. "Patsy Clark."

"Robert Williams."

"The expert on cowboys, right? The guy on TV."

"You saw my series on PBS."

She hooted. "I thought so!" She offered her hand, which Robert took. "Nice to meet you," she said.

"I'm not recognized all that often," he said, "so I must say I'm flattered. Are you a fan of the Old West?"

"I'll be honest with you, Bob…. Do your friends call you Bob?"

"Robert, actually."

"Good, I like to get a person's name right," she said. "As I was saying, *Robert*, all I know about cowboys is what I learned watching Clint Eastwood and Kevin Costner. The truth is, the only reason I watched your program is because my sister's kid, Jason, was staying with me for a couple of weeks, and he had to watch it for some school report or something like that."

"That's better than not having seen it at all, I suppose."

"Yeah." She sipped her drink. "Normally I don't go in for that stuff they show on PBS, but your show was pretty good, I got to admit."

"Glad you liked it."

Joe returned and, seeing Robert had company, gave him a conspiratorial wink.

"Ready for another drink?" Joe asked.

"Sure. And another for the lady."

Patsy beamed. "Thanks."

Joe went off to prepare their drinks.

"You're better looking in person," Patsy said, "and I thought you were kind of cute on TV."

"Thank you."

"Don't get the idea I'm some kind of groupie or anything," she said. "I'd have struck up a conversation if you were John Doe. I'm friendly that way."

"Glad you did."

She drank as Robert contemplated her. It was evident he was being presented an opportunity. The question was, did he wish to expend the energy to take advantage of it, or should he let it pass? He decided it was worth finding out just what she had in mind.

"Are you staying at the hotel?" he asked.

"Yes, me and my girlfriend, Lana. We're hairdressers in L.A.—Santa Monica, actually. We come to Hawaii every winter, each time to a different place. The Coral Reef is nice, but a little quiet."

"Not a place for singles."

"For sure. Are you married, by the way, Robert?"

"I was. My wife died four years ago."

"Sorry about that. She must have been young."

"She was."

Patsy shook her head, then gave him an inquisitive sideways glance. "You're not involved with anybody, then?"

"Not at the moment."

"I always like to ask that stuff right up front," she said. "Why beat around the bush, know what I mean?"

Joe brought their drinks and added them to Robert's tab. Patsy hurriedly sucked the last of the liquid from her old glass and picked up the fresh one. They touched glasses.

"To Clint and Kevin," Robert said.

"What the hell," Patsy rejoined. "To us."

"To us, then."

Robert subtly checked her out, measuring what she offered against the desire it evoked. "Are you involved with anyone?" he asked.

"I date, but nothing serious."

It was a place in the conversation where he could have said, "So have you eaten, have any plans for dinner?" but he hung back, not feeling sufficiently interested to make a pass. Not that she wouldn't have been fun to play with. Every indication was that Patsy was a pretty hot number. Maybe it was his age.

"There is one thing," she said.

Robert waited.

"Last night Lana and I met these guys in Lahaina. They're here from Phoenix for some convention or something. Anyway, she kind of liked one of them and they're supposed to come and take us to dinner tonight."

Robert could see she was foreclosing any invitation he might be considering. "I see."

"The reason I mention that," Patsy said, "is because I'm going to have to get up and run out of here any minute now and I didn't want you to think I was...you know...just flirting for the hell of it."

"I appreciate your thoughtfulness, Patsy."

She looked him over. "As a matter of fact, I'd invite you to dinner myself if it wasn't that I promised Lana."

"I'm flattered."

"You seem really nice," she said.

"So do you."

She bit her lip, reflecting on what she wanted to say. "I know this sounds forward, but Lana and I are leaving tomorrow, late afternoon, which means I can't even ask if you got plans for tomorrow night." She cleared her throat. "But I learned opportunities pass you by if you don't use them."

"Yes . . ."

"So, I was thinking that if you're the type who stays up, maybe I could meet you later after this dinner date I have to go on with Lana and her friends."

"You think it's worth the trouble?"

She shrugged. "I don't know about for you. It would be for me."

Robert found himself wanting to accommodate her, as much to reward her for her earnestness and courage as for the fact that she was sexy. He didn't make a practice of picking up women and, though it had happened a time or two, he wasn't much inclined to indulge in one-night stands.

"I was planning on going to my bungalow, ordering something from room service and kicking back," he said. "I'm not really a night owl, but I don't turn into a pumpkin at twelve, either."

Patsy laughed. "Tell you what, Robert, why don't I come by when we get back, and if you're up we can go out."

"That sounds fair enough."

"Which bungalow are you in?"

"Number twelve, closest to the water."

"I'll remember," she said, "twelve's my lucky number." She gave him a provocative smile, one that warmed his body. A frown crossed her face. "What time do you have, Robert?"

He consulted his watch. "It's nine-thirty."

"Oh, God, I've got to go. I'm supposed to meet Lana at the front entrance." She took a long drink through her straw, then bounced up from her stool. "Thanks for the drink. It's the highlight of my trip." Then she grinned. "So far, anyway."

Robert would have returned the compliment, but he was basically honest, and to have said the same in return would have been to have denied Christina. Had he been able to wave a magic wand and combine the two women, it would have been the trip of the century. "I enjoyed talking to you, Patsy."

She leaned over and gave him a kiss on the cheek. Then, arching a brow, she said in a sultry voice, "Leave a light on for me, cowboy."

Robert could only smile because he never made promises he wasn't sure he would keep. Still, he enjoyed the little show Patsy Clark put on as she strode from the bar. Reaching the door, she looked over her shoulder and blew him a kiss.

CHRISTINA LAY ON THE massage table, totally immersed in sensation. Her masseuse, a tiny Polynesian woman named Lia, had the strongest hands in the world. At the moment she was working the backs of her legs.

"This must be what heaven is like," Christina said. "Are you sure you aren't an angel?"

"No, miss. Just doing my job."

"Is it all the Mai Tais I've had or does everybody tell you you're a magician?"

"Some people like it more than others."

"Don't you dare tell my fiancé, but I'm afraid the rest of the evening is going to be an anticlimax."

Lia giggled. "I won't tell." She tittered. "Maybe."

"I guess that means I'm going to have to double your tip to keep my secret."

"No tip, miss. Everything on the house."

"You didn't flood our room and knock Bill over with a tray of food. Besides, you had to stay until after closing time to take care of me."

"The hotel is giving me a double tip. No problem."

"Oh," Christina said. "I feel better, then."

Lia began working Christina's feet. "You want another Mai Tai, miss?"

"Are you kidding? I won't be able to walk as it is."

She knew she was slurring her words, but she didn't care. She felt wonderful. Still, there would be hell to pay in the morning.

"Don't worry," Lia said. "I'm going to show you to your room. The assistant manager said you're getting a bungalow."

"Yes, but I don't have the key. I'll have to go to the desk first."

"No problem, miss. I'll send a towel boy up. Maybe I'll do it now so you don't have to wait."

"That would be nice. I'd rather not take a pratfall in the middle of the lobby."

Lia laughed. "What name is the room under?"

"William Roberts."

"Okay, I'll tell the towel boy. Excuse me, please."

Christina took a deep breath. She couldn't remember being this relaxed in her whole life. It had been a miserable day, but it was ending pleasantly enough.

"Hey, Sean," she heard the masseuse call out in the hall outside her cubicle. "I need you to go to the front desk for a room key. It's the bungalow for Robert Williams."

Christina was in a mellow daze. The girl's voice was almost like background music, yet there was something odd about what she just heard. But before she could decide what it was, Lia returned.

"Key's on the way, miss. As soon as I finish your feet, you can have your shower."

For the first time since the massage had begun, Christina made herself think ahead. Bill would be waiting, probably ready to make love. It was, after all, their honeymoon. Besides, he was the man she loved, the man she'd decided to spend her life with. So why wasn't she as eager to be with him as she ought to be?

If there was a real problem—if morning did not bring a genuine change in her perspective—then perhaps she'd have to rethink her priorities and decisions. But she would not spoil this, their first evening. She'd do her very best to love Bill, make it a wonderful time for them both. Sometimes when she was with him, it was hard to let go. Maybe all the Mai Tais would help. Lord knew, she'd had enough of them.

Twenty minutes later Christina was walking with Lia across the grounds of the Coral Reef. She was wrapped in a big fluffy terry robe that the hotel had given her. Lia had her by the arm, steadying her. Christina looked up at the star-studded sky.

"Oh, what a gorgeous night," she said.

"We have good weather all this week," Lia said.

They passed a couple coming toward them. Christina leaned close to Lia and whispered, "Do you think they knew I didn't have a stitch on under this robe?"

"No, miss," the masseuse said, giggling.

"Well, Bill's going to find out pretty damned quick, isn't he?"

Lia giggled again.

They'd come to the cluster of bungalows.

"This one's yours," she said as they turned off the side path to the door.

"Are you sure?" Christina said. "The lights are off."

Lia held up the key, showing her the number and pointing to the number on the door.

"Hmm. Do you think he got tired and went to sleep?"

The girl shrugged, then carefully stuck the key in the lock. She turned it, sliding the bolt free. The door opened a crack. It was dark inside.

"Maybe he got tired of waiting and went to sleep," Christina whispered. She extended her hand to Lia. "Well, thanks. I want you to know you're the best masseuse in the world."

"Thank you, miss," she whispered back. "Have a nice night."

"I'll do my part," Christina said, with a mischievous smile. She stepped inside and carefully closed the door. She half expected the lights to pop on then, but they didn't.

Though things seemed to be spinning, she managed to creep across the dark room to the bed. She could barely see Bill, but she could hear his soft breathing. He'd actually gone to sleep! On their wedding night! Well, the day after their almost wedding night.

Christina considered crawling into bed and going to sleep herself. After all, she was doing this more for him than herself. But if Bill had nodded off, it wasn't because he wasn't interested, it was because he was dead tired. On any other night she'd let him rest. But if there was one thing Christina would have bet her life on, it was that Bill would want her to awaken him so that they could make love.

Slipping the robe off her shoulders, she let it drop to the floor. Then she lifted the covers and crawled in bed. He moaned softly as she pressed her cool skin against his warm body.

"I know you're awfully tired," she cooed, "but if you wake up, I'll promise to make it worth your while."

Half-asleep, he ran his warm hand over her bare shoulder and down her back, groaning softly as he cupped her derriere, giving it a gentle squeeze. Christina rolled onto her back as the room started spinning. Bill, awake now, was right there, kissing her breasts. He swirled his tongue around her nipple, making it hard as a rock. At the same time he ran his hand down over the plane of her stomach and to the curls between her legs.

It wasn't as though he'd never touched her before. But there was something about his caress that seemed more deft, more sensuous than usual. Was it the alcohol, or was it Bill? Maybe, she decided, it was because this was their pseudo wedding night. That could be it.

Christina wormed her way closer, inhaling his fragrance, liking the new cologne he'd gotten in the hotel shop. She also liked the way he kissed her, as if he couldn't get enough of her, as if she was the air she needed to breathe. She returned each kiss, opening her mouth to him, until she felt she'd die if she didn't get more air. She pulled away to take a deep breath, but somehow that didn't help. The room was spinning.

Christina felt the bed whirl faster and faster. She fisted the sheets, trying to sort out reality from fantasy. Was this a sexy dream, or was Bill really doing all these marvelous things to her? Fingertips skittered across her skin. Lips nibbled at her ears, her neck, her breasts. She felt a raspy tongue skim her collarbone, then teasing kisses trailed across her stomach and to the juncture of her thighs.

She moaned, still not knowing whether to believe this was truly happening or not. But when a tongue seemed to tease her nub and then quickly swirl across her before dipping inside, she no longer cared. If this was an illusion, a hallucination, she didn't want it to end. Ever.

Never before had she felt so restless, so free. She wanted to go wherever her passion took her, to be whatever Bill wanted. She'd do anything, so long as all the wonderful sensations didn't stop. She found herself closing her eyes tightly and numbing her thoughts so that reality couldn't intrude. She wanted this game, this trance, this dizzy spell, to go on and on and on.

Her mind switched its focus to the warm and creamy feeling between her legs. The sensation she felt now was of a finger slipping inside her. As he stroked, Christina opened her eyes, unable to resist the temptation of finding out if this was real. Everything was dark, shadowy and bathed in the misty glow of her alcoholic haze. But two perceptions couldn't be denied—the sound of the pounding surf and the feel of his finger.

Christina knew she was on the verge of coming. That couldn't be her imagination. Could it? If Bill was a magician, a master of illusion, he was doing a damned good job of it. She grabbed his hand and pressed it against her, hard. She came like that, screaming her pleasure, gasping, writhing, out of control. She was still in the grip of her pleasure, still pulsing, when he parted her legs and moved over her.

He might have been a phantom, a figment of her drunken imagination, but she reached down to touch him anyway. He was smooth and hard. Heavy. She rubbed the tip of his sex against her opening, teasing herself and him. Never before had she been so overtly sexual. It had to be the Mai Tais.

He brushed her hand away and gently pushed the head of his sex into her an inch or so. Then he withdrew. Christina wiggled forward, trying to get closer, trying to make him go deeper, but he did the same thing again. Then again and again until she was moaning, begging for him to give her more. She wanted it this instant. Now.

Finally he plunged into her. Christina gasped. He paused for a moment to let her get used to him, then he began moving in long smooth strokes, entering her and drawing out. Slowly, ever so slowly, he built the pace. She spread her legs wider, but no matter how much she took of him, it wasn't enough.

When she was on the verge of another climax, she dug her nails into his buttocks and cried out. Bill plunged into her three or four times, much harder and faster than before, sending her over the edge. They both came then, with the room spinning around them. Christina was so dizzy, she wasn't sure if she was clinging to Bill out of desire, or a need to keep from falling. But she no longer cared which. Nothing mattered except their pleasure.

It was a long time before she stopped pulsing. Christina took a deep breath, trying to ground herself in reality. Bill didn't move until she absently nibbled his neck. Then he brushed her hair out of her face, kissed her moist brow and her ear. And when he rolled to his side, he held her tightly and took her with him so he could stay inside her. She fell asleep that way, still not sure how much of her pleasure had been real, and how much was in her mind.

5

IT WAS DAWN and Christina was in misery. Her head hurt at the thought of opening her eyes. She tried to summon the will to get up and go to the bathroom, but her head bothered her more than her bladder. So she decided to give herself another five minutes in bed.

She could only recall one other occasion when she'd had a hangover. It was while she was still in college. She was at the wedding of her best friend, Molly Wilkerson. After Molly and Jack had left on their honeymoon, all the bridesmaids had retired with a magnum of champagne for a party of their own. Christina had been twenty-one and she'd gotten drunk for the only time in her life.

Until last night.

She lay very still. Her head throbbed with each beat of her heart. Maybe, if she tried to relax, the pain would lessen.

Despite her misery, pleasurable details of the night before started streaming into her consciousness. For a second it seemed as though she'd dreamed it, but then she realized it had actually happened. Bill had been fantastic. Incredible.

They'd made love twice more during the night. Never before had Bill turned her on so much. Why, she wondered, had he saved it for their honeymoon? Lord, she hoped it wasn't the Mai Tais because she certainly didn't plan on getting high every time they made love in the future.

Christina was suddenly aware of the silence. Bill wasn't snoring. Was he up?

She was on her side of the bed, facing the sliding glass door. Reaching back with her hand, she touched his leg. He moaned softly. She scooted against him for the pleasure of the contact, and when she squeezed his thigh, she was surprised at how firm and muscular it felt.

Bill snuggled closer, wedging his body against her. He didn't usually cuddle, and this unexpected show of affection came as a surprise. Sliding an arm around her, he cupped her breast and semiconsciously kissed her shoulder.

Christina opened her eyes for the first time, squinting at the light filtering through the shutters. It was bright enough to send a surge of pain through her brain. She closed her eyes again. Bill gently squeezed her breast, then ran his thumb over her nipple, making it harden. It was a mixed blessing because her rising heartbeat made her head hurt worse.

Deciding she couldn't put the trip to the bathroom off any longer, she removed his hand from her breast. Maybe a couple of aspirin and a hot shower would revive her to the point where she would want to make love again. This was, after all, a honeymoon. And if last night was any indication of the way things would be from here on out, she was all for it. Bill had been a whole new man last night.

Christina started to get up, but Bill gave a semiconscious growl of disapproval and moved his hand. As he did, she regarded it. Why did his arm look strange? There was no coating of thick dark hair. What the hell was going on? Christina bolted upright and slowly turned toward the man lying beside her.

It wasn't Bill! She screamed out in horror and shrank away, clutching at the sheets, struggling to cover herself and retreat at the same time.

The man blinked awake, shock registering on his face, the same as hers. "What are you doing in my bed?" she screamed, moving still farther away. "Where's Bill?"

The man shook his head, dumbfounded. He peered around the room, squinting. "What the hell . . ."

"How did you get in here?" she gasped, fighting her panic. "What have you done to Bill?"

The man stared at her with utter disbelief. He sat up, scratching his head. "What are *you* doing here, Christina?"

Her mouth dropped open. "You know my name!"

"Well, I . . . I . . ."

"Get out!" she screamed at the top of her lungs. "Get out of here immediately! I'm calling the police. Get out!"

He put a hand on his hip, annoyance registering on his face. "Wait a minute. This is *my* room."

"What do you mean, *your* room?" She clutched the sheet to her throat.

"This is my bungalow," he said. "But how did you..."

She watched as he tried to calculate what might have happened. Her mouth dropped open still wider as she, too, played back the events of the night before. *This* man was the one she'd made love with. Not Bill. *This stranger.*

"Oh, my God," she said under her breath. "*You* were in this bed last night. You were the one who . . . Oh, my God."

In that instant, the whole scenario fell into place in her mind. The unknown became the known. The comprehensible world suddenly became incomprehensible. She wanted the earth to open up and swallow her. She'd slept with this stranger—made love with him.

"You took advantage of me," she muttered, as much in disbelief as horror.

"Hold on a minute. I didn't take advantage of anybody. *You* got into *my* bed last night."

"I had too many Mai Tais!" she cried, her revulsion laced with indignation.

"I know that, but I thought you were someone else."

"What?"

"I thought you were someone else."

She shook her head with disbelief. "This is not possible. I couldn't have made love with you. I don't even know you!"

He stared at her soberly. Then a slight smile began to play at the corners of his mouth. "It's true we haven't been formally introduced, but we aren't exactly strangers anymore."

Her eyes flashed. "This isn't funny! In fact, it's rape! You took advantage of me under false pretenses. I was drunk out of my mind. That's rape!"

"Hold it right there. I didn't take advantage of you. You took advantage of me. I was sound asleep, in my own bed, and you came in and seduced me."

"I thought you were Bill!" she snapped.

"That's hardly my fault."

"You should have said something."

"I told you, I thought you were somebody else, a woman I met last night."

"Yeah? Well, if that's true, how come you know my name? I heard you call me Christina."

"That's because I was in the bar when . . . Bill . . . had his accident. I witnessed the whole thing. I heard him call you Christina."

"See! You *did* know who I was. You knew I thought I was going to bed with Bill."

"No, I thought you were Patsy. She came on to me in the bar late last night, after you'd left for dinner. I figured she'd decided to pay a late-night call."

"You mean you thought I was some *barfly*."

"I wouldn't say she was a barfly. No, she definitely wasn't a barfly. I didn't even intend to—"

"Please," she exclaimed, the utter horror of it all seizing her, "I don't want to hear. Your sex life doesn't interest me. I don't even want to know what you were thinking."

"I'm trying to tell you it was an innocent mistake."

Christina couldn't look at him any longer. Instead, she began calculating the implications. Bill. Good Lord! What must he be thinking? What would happen when he found out?

"What I want to know is how you got in here," the man said.

She looked at him, really seeing him for the first time. He was naked from the waist up, the sheet draped discreetly over his lap. His chest was a thick mat of brown hair. Bill had a few hairs on his chest, but not many. How could she not have noticed the difference?

Christina turned scarlet, recalling all the things they'd done during the night. Embarrassed, she had to look away. She couldn't deal with this.

"Did you have a key?" he asked.

Christina, still clutching the sheet to her throat, pulled her knees to her chest. "No," she said without looking at him, "the masseuse let me in. She had a key. I hadn't been to the room before. It was dark when I entered. I assumed . . ." She felt sick. "Oh, God. How could this have happened?"

For several moments he didn't say anything. Then, "Well . . . there's no real harm done."

"What do you mean, there's no harm done?" she snapped. "I slept with you, and I don't even know you! Until I woke up in your bed, I wouldn't have recognized you if you'd walked up and slapped me in the face!"

"Look, let's not panic," he said.

"Not panic?" She glared. "Easy for you to say, maybe, but I allowed you to make love with me and I don't even know your name!"

"It's Robert Williams."

"*I don't care what your name is!* Don't you see that's not the point? We're sitting four feet from each other, completely naked, and we're total strangers. I might as well have picked your name out of a hat!"

"I don't have any social diseases," he said, "if that's what you're worried about."

"Social diseases?" she cried. "Oh, my God!"

"Well, I'd think you'd be glad."

She closed her eyes, certain she was going to break into tears. "Social diseases," she muttered under her breath. "How can you talk about social diseases when I've just had the most embarrassing and humiliating and devastating experience of my life?"

"Look," Robert said, "this is a big shock to me, too. After all, I didn't exactly expect to see you here, either. But what's done is done. We'll just have to deal with it."

Christina looked at him from the corner of her eye, disbelieving. "How can you be so logical at a time like this? This is not a time for logic, Mr.... Mr.... What did you say your name was?"

"Robert Williams. Call me Robert, if you like."

She rolled her eyes. "*Robert*, we are in the middle of a disaster, a catastrophe! I'm here on my honeymoon and I've made love with the wrong man. How will I be able to live with myself, or with Bill? What will I tell him? He's probably looking for me, thinking I've been kidnapped or something, and you're introducing yourself, assuring me you don't have any social diseases and telling me what's done is done like I'm just supposed to forget it."

"Personally, I'll never forget it."

She gave him another withering glare. "Will you cut the smart remarks, please. This is my life we're discussing!"

"What, pray tell, do you expect me to say? That I'm glad? That I couldn't be more pleased? That you were a great lay?"

She looked at him sullenly, hating what had happened.

"Well?" he said.

"I don't want you to say anything. I just wish you'd disappear. I wish this had never happened and that I didn't have to look at you."

"Well, it has happened, Christina, so let's deal with it as best we can. I'll speak with your husband, if you think that'll help. If he loves you, I'm sure he'll understand. If you made a mistake, it was getting drunk. Surely he'll forgive you. This isn't the Victorian age, after all."

"Bill's not my husband."

"What?"

"Bill's not my husband. We're engaged. In fact, we were supposed to be married the day before yesterday, but it didn't happen because . . . Oh, never mind. It's a long story, and besides, it doesn't matter."

"You're not married," he said.

Christina saw the shock on his face turn to delight. "But we're the same as married," she said quickly. "It's only a technicality."

"You're on your honeymoon, but technically you aren't married?"

"I know it sounds strange, but it's perfectly logical. You'll just have to take my word for it because I have no intention of explaining my personal life to you."

He chuckled. "Not after only one date, anyway."

"There you go again, making light of it. Don't you see that my future with Bill is hanging in the balance? How would you feel if you were in his shoes?"

"Forgive me for saying so, but I'd never have allowed this to happen if I were in his shoes, because you wouldn't have been out of my sight long enough to stumble into another man's bed."

His words sobered her. It was not what she wanted to hear. "Bill's the innocent victim in this," she said. "I'm responsible for what's happened, not him."

"So what are you going to do now?"

"Go find my fiancé. But first I have to go to the bathroom. Would you mind turning your head so I can get out of bed and put something on?"

He turned his back to her and Christina slipped from the bed. Seeing the bathrobe she'd left on the floor, she snatched it up and hurriedly slipped it on. The sudden exertion made her woozy. For a moment she thought she might be sick. With all the excitement, she'd forgotten just how rotten she felt. She sat on the edge of the bed to keep from collapsing to the floor.

"Are you all right?"

She glanced back at Robert, who looked genuinely concerned.

"Yes, just a bit shaky. Hangover." She put her head in her hands. "I'll never drink again. Not a drop."

"Is there anything I can do to help?"

Christina got to her feet. "No, I'll be all right." She got up and started for the bathroom, then stopped. "Maybe there is something. Call the desk and find ⟨ what bungalow Bill's in. And if they've got the police looking for me, tell them I'm okay. Tell them . . . No, wait, maybe you'd better not say anything. Just find out where Bill Roberts is."

After she went to the bathroom, Christina splashed cold water on her face. As she looked at herself in the mirror, she saw that her hair was a tangled mess; she had shadows under her eyes and looked puffy and pale.

She cupped running water from the faucet in her hand and took a drink. When the cold hit her churning gut she nearly threw up. Her head was killing her. She needed an aspirin.

Christina went to the door with the intent of asking Robert if he had something she could take for her head. But when she opened the door, she saw him standing naked across the room, his back to her, turning the sleeves of his robe right side out. She started to close the door, then stopped. She couldn't help but admire his lean, muscular physique. He was, after all, the man who had done all those marvelous things to her the night before.

Her eye traced the line from his broad shoulders down to his narrow waist and hips, lingering on his tight buns and powerful legs. Robert Williams had a great body, and Lord, did he ever know how to use it. But drooling over him was hardly the thing to be doing. She had to keep things in perspective.

She quietly closed the door and let her forehead fall against the smooth, cool wood as her mind rolled back over the previous night. She could almost hear her cries of pleasure, her throaty gasps and moans as he'd thrust into her. She remembered the wonderful tingling she'd felt as he brought her to climax. The recollection made her tremble.

Much as she wanted to, Christina knew she couldn't say it had been Bill she'd made love with the night before—even in spirit. True, she'd thought it was Bill at the time, but not the Bill Roberts of her experience. The man who'd given her so much pleasure was a master of lovemaking, a lover of extraordinary accomplishment.

She turned and looked at his things on the vanity— his razor, deodorant, toothbrush, cologne. He was a total stranger. How had she made love with him and not known that she was with someone other than Bill? Had she been *that* drunk?

Minutes earlier she'd brushed aside his assurances that he was free of disease, but what if that wasn't true? If last night he'd thought he was making love to some woman he'd only just met, who might he have been with the night before? Again, she quailed at the thought. This was a potential tragedy of tremendous proportions. And she still had Bill to deal with.

Christina took a peek inside the shaving kit on the corner of the vanity. She found a small bottle of aspirin. She helped herself to a couple of tablets, deciding it was a small liberty. After running her fingers through her hair, she returned to the main room, relieved that Robert Williams was wearing a bathrobe. He was sitting on the bed, just hanging up the phone. He glanced her way and smiled.

"Good news," he said. "There's no frantic manhunt for you in progress. I didn't ask directly, but it's possible you haven't been missed."

Christina was surprised. She approached the bed, pulling her robe closed at the neck. "But what about Bill?"

"It's still fairly early, you know. Maybe he fell asleep and hasn't awakened yet. It could be he hasn't discovered you never returned to the room."

"Where's our bungalow?"

"Right across the walk. Number thirteen."

Christina felt a brief twinge of panic. To think Bill had been only a few feet away the whole time.

"I'll be leaving then," she said, feeling odd. How did you say goodbye to someone you'd made love with by accident?

Robert got up and moved around the bed. His expression was more concerned than threatening, but Christina was wary just the same. A strange, panicky feeling gripped her.

"Look, Christina, I'm awfully sorry about last night," Robert said.

His voice had a pleasant, reassuring quality, but she took half a step back anyway. It was almost as if she was afraid he'd touch her. "So am I," she stammered. "And between us, I suppose I'm more to blame than you. I got into *your* bed, not the other way around."

"Forgive me if this sounds insensitive, but I'm not sorry. I mean, I'm not sorry for my own sake. A case of mistaken identity or not, it was an incredible night."

The comment caught her completely off guard. Was it a compliment, or a totally insensitive remark? She chose the latter. "I don't know how you have the gall to say that."

"I meant no disrespect. If I have a regret it's over any pain you may have suffered. But I'd like to think that at the time it was as enjoyable for you as it was for me."

She turned bright red. But there was nothing she could say to that. Nothing at all. "I'm leaving now," she muttered.

Robert extended his hand. "Can we part friends? I want you to know that as far as I'm concerned, it can be our secret. I'm not going to say a word to anyone. God knows, I don't want this to be a bigger problem for you than it already is."

She looked at his hand but didn't take it. "I'm definitely not looking forward to telling Bill what happened." She turned and started toward the door. "I'd better go. The sooner I get back, the better."

She wanted to say something more, but she didn't know what. Robert Williams spoke instead. "If you do tell him about last night, Christina, let Bill know he's a very, very fortunate man. I'd trade places with him in a flash."

With that, she fumbled for the doorknob, stepped outside, and quietly closed the door. She could hear the crashing surf. She looked up at the early-morning sky. The air was fresh and sweet. For a moment she savored it, trying not to think of her throbbing head.

She looked at the bungalow across the way. It seemed quiet, undisturbed. Perhaps Bill was sleeping. Could it be her absence would go undiscovered? It was possible. But even if she didn't tell him, how would she ever forget?

6

CHRISTINA OPENED the door to the sound of Bill's snoring. She found him lying on the bed in his boxer shorts, sleeping peaceful as a baby.

Next to the bed was an ice bucket with an open bottle of champagne. A glass with some wine left in it was on the bedside table. The tale was obvious—Bill had ordered the champagne, grown tired of waiting for her, had a glass to relax, then had fallen asleep. Which meant he was oblivious to her infidelity.

Ironically, she was almost as annoyed that her absence had gone unnoticed as she was relieved that it had. Almost. Yet how could she blame him for falling asleep after the day he'd had?

Christina stared at him lying there, unaware of her betrayal. The fact that it was unintentional seemed not to matter. Tears came to her eyes. She felt wretched. It wasn't just that she'd been unfaithful, it was that making love with Robert had been fabulous. That made it much worse because she knew now that all the nights she'd shared with Bill paled by comparison. In reality, he fell far short as a lover. That couldn't be ignored.

Of course, a man's prowess in bed had nothing to do with love. What truly mattered was the person he was.

Still, she wanted to be fulfilled by him in every way. How could she be with Bill in the future and not resent it when he couldn't live up to Robert's standard? Of course, it wouldn't be fair to hold Bill responsible for that, but would she anyway?

Christina stared at the untouched pillow next to Bill. She considered getting under the covers and lying there until he awoke, but she couldn't bring herself to do it. The Bill Roberts of reality—the one snoring softly— suddenly seemed undesirable to her, even in his innocence. She yearned for the Bill she thought she'd been with last night, the one who'd made her feel passionately alive.

Christina's anxiety made her head begin to throb. She felt sick at heart, wanting to believe that her doubts would pass, but unsure if they would. She sat in the chair by the bed to think. Given that she'd just left one man's bed for another's, it was only natural that she'd feel confused and anxious. This was temporary, she told herself. Robert Williams would soon fade from memory, just as every other man she'd known had.

After all, it wasn't like she hadn't had decent sex before. She'd been around enough to know that Bill wasn't an especially accomplished lover. Certainly not the best she'd had. Since that hadn't bothered her before, why now?

Maybe the problem was she wasn't sure what to do. It was one thing to have been with another man months before she and Bill had gotten together. It was another entirely to have made love with a stranger on what was, for all intents and purposes, their wedding night. The timing was what was so horrible.

Did she tell Bill, or did she lie? That was the issue. Was it a greater kindness to spare him, or did she owe him the truth, however painful?

If she'd slept with Robert knowingly, it would speak to feelings for Bill, something he had a right to know about. But given the fact it was an accident, did her obligations change?

Christina's father had once told her people had a right to know about things that impacted their lives. Maybe that was the right standard. If she could put what had happened behind her, go on with her life, then maybe Bill didn't need to know. But if she ended up scarred by the incident, then maybe she'd owe him the truth. That was the solution, she decided—to wait and see.

Having resolved the matter to her satisfaction, at least for the time being, Christina got up. She went to the bed and dented the pillow with her fist. Then she carefully rumpled the bedding on her side and stole off to the bathroom for a shower.

Fifteen minutes later she was standing at the mirror in a fresh white terry cloth bathrobe, running her comb through her wet hair, when the bathroom door opened. Bill, a woebegone expression on his face, slumped against the doorframe as he looked at her mournfully.

"Chris, honey, I'm sorry," he said. "Will you ever forgive me?"

"Forgive you? What are you talking about, Bill?"

"For falling asleep like that. Jeez, it was our wedding night, practically, and what do I do? I fall asleep before you even get in bed. I wouldn't blame you if you killed me."

"Don't be silly, Bill. When I left the spa, I was so drunk I could barely walk. I'm the one who's ashamed. I've given up drink, believe me."

He smiled. "Then you aren't mad at me?"

"No, of course I'm not. But I am in misery. I have the worst hangover known to man . . . or woman."

Bill slipped his arms around her. They stood there, holding each other. Christina's eyes filled with tears as she rubbed his shoulder, feeling like a traitor.

"Sweetheart," he said, "I can't tell you how glad I am that you're so forgiving. I don't deserve you. You know that, don't you?"

"Bill, please don't say that."

He pulled back so he could see her, immediately noticing the tears in her eyes. "You *are* upset."

She shook her head. "No, not at all."

"Then why are you crying?"

She bit her lip. "Because I feel dreadful."

"Hey, I've had a few hangovers in my time, too. Tropical drinks can kill you. I should have warned you about them."

"I'm a big girl, Bill. I should be able to take care of myself. My dad always used to say, if you make your own bed, you'd better be prepared to lie in it."

He took her chin in his hand and gave her his wide, happy grin, the one she associated with him. "Speaking of beds, do you have any plans for the next few hours?" he asked, twitching his eyebrows. "The champagne's flat, but I could order some orange juice from room service."

There was nothing surprising about the suggestion, but Christina's stomach clenched at the thought of going to bed with him just then. She knew it would happen eventually, but she was not up to it now—emotionally or physically.

"Bill," she said, touching his arm, "I feel sick as a dog. It wouldn't be pleasant for either of us."

He considered that. Then, embarrassed, he said, "Of course you don't. It was selfish of me to suggest it."

"No, it wasn't selfish. I feel terrible for letting myself get in this condition. It's unfair to you."

"Don't be silly, Chris. I understand. Honest."

He sounded sincere enough, but she could tell he was masking his disappointment.

"Are you sure?"

"Yes," he said, trying to sound chipper. "Let's spend the day recuperating, and tonight if you feel up to it, we can have a party then. And if you're still not feeling well, we'll make it tomorrow. After all, we've got forty or fifty years to find the right occasion."

Christina chuckled, patting his cheek. "You're a saint. I want you to know how grateful I am that you're so sweet."

Bill kissed her, pulling her against him. She tried to return the affection, but strangely, she found it difficult. No flood of emotion welled up, no deep feelings of love. The kiss felt dead. How could that be? They were supposed to marry two days ago, but she felt nothing. Nothing. A tremor went through her, but she tried not to let her anxiety show.

After releasing her, Bill grinned again, not having noticed her lack of response. "You're a gem, sweetheart," he said. "You truly are. Priceless."

The comment brought more tears to her eyes. She felt so unworthy. How could she let Bill love her, and how could she love him after what happened? Would things ever be the same again?

"Listen, while you finish your hair, I'll jump in the shower," Bill said. "Then afterward why don't we have a look at the room service menu? They say one of the great pleasures in this world is to sit out on the deck of an oceanfront bungalow at the Coral Reef in Maui, drink freshly squeezed orange juice, eat a pastry and watch the waves come rolling in from the blue Pacific."

"Okay," Christina said, dabbing her eyes, "I'm game. Whatever you want to do is fine with me."

ROBERT WILLIAMS towel-dried his hair, then leaned on the vanity, staring at his face in the mirror. The night with Christina had transformed him. He'd been reborn as a man and as a lover.

Things like this did not happen without cause. It had been a miracle. Last evening he'd seen a goddess, worshipped her from afar, only to awaken to discover that he'd spent the night making love to her. It wasn't a dream. It had actually occurred. The woman had climbed into his bed and they'd made wild, wonderful, passionate love.

When she'd first awakened him, he'd assumed it was Patsy, from the bar. But at some level, he'd known it wasn't. The hair had been wrong, and her manner was different, even drunk. Those fabulous long legs had to be the ones he'd spied from the garden. Deep in his soul, he'd known it was Christina. He hadn't stopped to ask why it was happening, or even if it was true. He'd just wanted to cling to the fantasy the way a dreamer longed to cling to his dream.

The trouble was, morning had come. The experience had been real, but it was over. Dream or memory? What difference did it make if that was all he'd ever have of her? Of course, he was damn lucky to have had the experience at all. What man wouldn't be?

And yet, he couldn't help being frustrated. Christina was much more in his mind than just an attractive woman he'd had sex with. She was special, the fulfillment of an incredible fantasy. The simple truth was, he didn't want to let go.

Things were very different now from when he'd admired her from afar. Not only had they made love, but he'd learned that she wasn't married. That changed things completely, at least in his mind. It didn't matter that she was engaged. Until she was another man's wife, she was fair game.

The trouble was, he wan't exactly her favorite person right now. How would he get past that? Was there any point in trying?

Still staring into the mirror, Robert wondered what the hell had gotten into him. He didn't know a damned thing about Christina except that she was on a honeymoon but wasn't married. He would be leaving Maui in two more days. What was he thinking?

That he actually could have some kind of future with this woman?

Robert dried his hair, slipped on a pair of shorts and a Hawaiian shirt, then called room service. After straightening the room a little, he wandered onto the deck to look at the ocean.

It was a bright, sunny morning. The air was fragrant with the clean smell of the sea. Robert took a deep breath. He loved the tropical air almost as much as the mountain air at home. For a moment he stared at a sailboat a mile or so offshore, then he turned and looked at the adjoining bungalow.

He wondered what had happened when Christina returned. Had she told Bill what happened? If so, had he raged? Anxiety shot through Robert at the thought of her dealing with it alone. He'd been her partner in crime, and yet he was helpless to do anything to help her. Her sole wish with regard to him was that he would disappear. She'd wanted to forget what had happened.

Even as he was wrestling with the problem, the sliding glass door at the bungalow next door opened and Bill Roberts stepped onto the deck. He went to the railing and stared out to sea. Robert studied him, trying to decide if Bill was a man in pain.

There were no obvious signs of consternation. If anything, he looked relaxed and at ease. Robert guessed the night's events had gone undiscovered.

Just then Bill glanced his way. "Good morning!" he called cheerily. "Beautiful day, isn't it?"

"Perfect," Robert replied.

If there was any uncertainty about what Bill knew or didn't know, it had been laid to rest. Robert was relieved.

"I'm from Seattle," Bill said. "To us, rain is a way of life, especially in winter. You don't even notice it after a while. But you come to Hawaii, and you see this sun, and it's like a whole different world."

"I know what you mean," Robert said.

"Where are you from?"

"Santa Fe."

"Ah, New Mexico. I don't know a lot about that part of the world. Born and raised in the Pacific Northwest, myself."

"Nice up that way," Robert said. His mind started turning. If Bill was from Seattle, chances were Christina was, as well. "Matter of fact, I'm going to be headed to Portland, then on to Seattle in a couple of days."

"Oh, really? Business or pleasure?"

"Business," Robert said.

"What line of work you in, if you don't mind me asking?"

"I'm a writer. A historian, actually."

"You teach?"

"Used to. Lately I've been doing some things for public television," Robert said.

"No kidding. My fiancée is in television. She writes and produces children's programs for the PBS affiliate in Seattle."

Robert was shocked. That made Christina practically a colleague. What a coincidence. "Interesting," he said.

"I'm sure Chris would like to meet you," Bill said. "Especially if you'll be coming to the station." He laughed. "Small world, eh?"

"Yes, isn't it?"

"My fiancée and I are on sort of a premarriage honeymoon," Bill said. "The wedding got delayed, but we decided to come here anyway. How about you? Are you with your wife?"

Robert shook his head. "No, I came alone."

Bill nodded, leaning on the rail. "I'm in coffee myself," he said. "I own the biggest chain of coffeehouses in the Pacific Northwest. We're in Tacoma, Portland, Vancouver, Eugene, Spokane and half a dozen other places. Opening a new store every couple of months. I plan on taking a good look at California next. Seattle's a good coffee town, though, believe me. We've had a great run of luck."

"Fascinating," Robert said.

Just then Christina stepped out onto the deck. She was in white shorts and a green tank top. Robert's heart skipped a beat at the sight of her. She was as stunning as she'd been the night before, though now that there was some history between them, the image was completely different.

"Sweetheart," Bill said to her, "guess what? Our neighbor is in public television, just like you."

Christina turned and looked in Robert's direction. First dismay, then near-panic, registered on her face. She seemed horrified.

"I'm sorry, I didn't get your name," Bill called to him.

"Robert Williams," he replied.

"No kidding. Mine's William Roberts."

Bill laughed and so did Robert. Christina didn't seem amused in the least.

"We're sort of mirror images, aren't we?" Robert said affably.

Bill chuckled, nodding. Christina's expression, by contrast, had grown even darker.

"Robert, allow me to introduce my fiancée, Christina Cavanaugh," Bill said. "Chris, this is Mr. Williams from Santa Fe."

"Hello," she said, giving him a withering look.

"Nice to meet you, Ms. Cavanaugh," he replied. "Bill tells me you write and produce children's programs for public TV."

"Yes I do." Her frown was obviously intended to signal her disapproval of his friendliness. The look on her face screamed, *Go away! Can't you understand I don't want to look at you?*

"Robert's coming to the station in Seattle on business soon," Bill told her. "He's a historian."

"How interesting," she said. Her eyes repudiated her words.

"What is it, exactly, that you do for PBS?" Bill asked.

"My field's the Old West. I've done one series for the network already. At the moment I'm touring, promoting the next series, doing interviews with the print media, talking to station execs. It's a pain, though. What I enjoy doing is writing."

"Chris is the same," Bill said, putting his arm around her shoulders, "aren't you, sweetheart?"

Christina nodded. Bill turned then, looking back into the bungalow.

"Oops. Somebody's at the door," he said. "Must be our breakfast. I'll get it."

Bill disappeared inside. Christina turned to Robert, her eyes flashing.

"Why are you doing this?"

"Doing what?"

"Intruding into my life. Haven't you done enough damage already?"

"Hey, I'm on my deck enjoying the morning air. Bill struck up a conversation with me, not the other way around. It's not my fault that he's friendly."

"Well, you don't have to encourage him, do you?"

He shook his head, signaling his disgust. "You're being unreasonable, Christina. You consider what happened last night a disaster . . . that's clear. But life goes on. You'd be better off accepting that."

She glanced into the bungalow. "I'll worry about my life, Mr. Williams. You worry about yours."

Robert shrugged. "Whatever you say, *sweetheart*."

She sent another dark look his way. Just then there was a knock at the door of his bungalow. Robert went inside. It was the room service waiter. He had the waiter take it out onto his deck for an open-air breakfast.

Robert glanced over and saw that his neighbors were doing the same. Christina had positioned herself with her back to him. Out of sight, out of mind, evidently. That was unfortunate, he decided, but understandable. After all, she had a fiancé, whereas he was unattached.

He signed the bill, sending the waiter on his way. Then he sat down to eat.

Bill looked over and, seeing that he was about to eat, too, called out to him, *"Bon appétit."*

"Likewise," Robert replied, waving.

He began drinking his orange juice, having positioned himself so that he could see Christina. The sight of her long auburn hair made him feel wistful, weak. He recalled the sweet scent of her hair, the fresh taste of her mouth, all the little sounds she'd made as he plunged into her, and then her cries of pleasure when she came. He'd known this woman intimately, and yet she wasn't his. He meant nothing to her.

He couldn't be objective, and heaven knew he had little evidence to go on, but it seemed to him Bill Roberts was a very different type of man from him. How had she confused them in bed? How was it that she wanted to marry this jovial coffee king who seemed so completely wrong for a writer, someone who made her living in a creative field? It had to be because of Bill's money. Why else?

Robert knew he was jealous. He watched them, listening to them laughing, wondering how she'd so easily dismissed what had happened between them. Mistake or not, how could she discount what they'd shared? Had he completely lost perspective, or had she?

Robert nibbled on a pastry as the waves rolled in. He tried to ignore the goddess on the adjoining deck, but he couldn't get her out of his mind. Now that he knew something about her life, he yearned to know more, much more. As writers, they undoubtedly had a lot in common. He hoped to God he'd get the chance to find out what.

7

AFTER BREAKFAST Bill asked Christina if she wanted to walk on the beach. She told him that she did, and went in to put on some sunscreen and get the floppy hat she'd bought in the hotel shop the previous evening. She had to be careful in the sun, though she'd always loved the feel of the heat on her skin.

While she was in the bathroom getting ready, Bill got a call saying their luggage was back in Honolulu and would be delivered to them within a few hours. Christina was pleased—not that losing it permanently would have been a disaster, but she took it as an omen of things returning to normal.

"You see," Bill said, coming to the door, "this will turn out to be a great trip yet."

On an impulse Christina went over and gave him a hug. "Do you really think so?"

"Yes, definitely," he said.

Bill was in a good mood. On the one hand, she was glad of that. On the other, it made her feel even more guilty. It was probably better that he was oblivious to her misadventure, because if he knew that their "neighbor" had made love with her all night, his outlook would undoubtedly be quite different. Better he be blissfully ignorant, she told herself, rather than bitter and suspicious.

There was a disadvantage to that, though. It meant that she had to carry the emotional burden alone. And that in turn meant she had no good reason for being in a funk. The hangover excuse wouldn't last forever. She'd soon have to get into a more loving frame of mind, or be prepared to explain why she wasn't.

"How's the head?" Bill asked as she got her hat from the closet.

"Still throbbing, but I'll survive."

She got her sunglasses and they went onto the deck. Christina discreetly looked over at Robert Williams's bungalow. He wasn't in sight. She was relieved. It was bad enough having slept with him, but the thought of having to see him around all the time made her quail. Maybe he'd gone to play golf, or find the woman he'd mistaken her for. That would be a blessing.

The news he would be coming to Seattle had not sat well with her. Of course, that didn't mean she'd be seeing him. They had no reason to meet. Still, the thought of him at the station was hitting a little too close to home.

Bill guided her past Robert's bungalow. "Funny that our neighbor's a writer and works in public television, too, isn't it?" he said.

"Yeah, small world."

"You never heard of him?"

"Not really."

She hadn't seen his series, though now that the issue had been raised, his name and face did seem familiar. Her first glimpse of him that morning had come under such dramatic circumstances that she'd hardly been in any condition to run him through her memory bank. Undoubtedly, though, she'd seen footage from his series, and perhaps had run across publicity pieces, as well.

"Seems like an okay guy," Bill said as they strolled on through the palm trees and toward the water. "Of course, our conversation was brief." He chuckled. "But I may have been prejudiced somewhat by his performance last night."

Christina whipped her head in Bill's direction. "What?"

His expression was placid. There was no visible indication he knew.

"Wh-What do you mean?" she stammered, her throat tightening.

"While I was waiting for you to return from the spa last night, I was listening to him at play. He had some woman over there in absolute ecstasy. You should have heard them, Chris. Either he was putting on a hell of a performance—or she was."

Christina turned bright crimson. If Bill had looked at her, the jig would have been up. She turned toward the ocean, hoping the sea breeze would cool her skin.

"I sort of found it inspiring," Bill went on. "They sounded like they were having such a good time, it made me eager for you to get back." He slipped his arm around her waist and gave it a squeeze. "My mistake was having that champagne."

Christina suddenly felt sick again. "We all made our share of mistakes last night," she said mournfully. "But it's over and done with. We just have to concentrate on the future and forget about Robert Williams."

"Actually, I was thinking it might be nice to invite him to have a drink with us," Bill said.

"No!"

He looked at her strangely.

"What I mean is, why mix business with pleasure?" she improvised. "I don't want to talk television on my honeymoon, for heaven's sake."

Bill shrugged. "It just seemed like he'd be an interesting guy. But if you don't want to, fine."

Christina took his arm as they neared the water. The warm sun on her back felt good, the sea breeze was pleasant and balmy. She looked out at the blue-green water, and what should pop into her mind but Robert Williams. He was the last person she wanted to think about, but he was right there, in the forefront of her thoughts.

Bill began talking about the things they could do that day. She half listened as he talked about the golf course, the shopping, the places they could go. But as he talked, her mind kept tripping back to the previous night. During those hours of bliss, Bill had seemed larger than life, the kind of lover she'd always dreamed of. And now that she knew she'd been with someone else, the man she intended to marry seemed lesser than he'd been before.

Christina hated herself for thinking that way. Sex wasn't everything. With many couples, it was a relatively minor part of their relationship. But now that she thought about it, she wasn't absolutely sure that sex was the issue. Perhaps this was really about passion. She hadn't wanted to admit it before, but maybe her problems with Bill went deeper than the physical. Maybe she had talked herself into marriage without caring for Bill the way she should.

"Christina?"

"Huh?" Then she realized he'd asked her a question and she hadn't paid attention to him. "Oh, sorry, my mind was wandering. What did you say?"

"I said, how about if we rent some clubs and play a little golf?"

"Oh, I'm not much of a player, as you know, Bill."

"You only played with me that one time and it was raining. We've got beautiful, sunny weather today. Come on, Chris, give it a try."

"All right, Bill, if it'll make you happy."

AN HOUR LATER they walked out of the pro shop, outfitted and ready to go. The problem was, the first available tee time wasn't for an hour and they were lucky to have gotten that time slot. "It doesn't matter," Bill said, "we'll have a beer while we wait."

"Or in my case, a glass of ice tea," Christina said.

Bill got their rented golf cart and loaded their clubs. He parked the cart by the clubhouse and they headed for the coffee shop. As they walked through the doors, they saw Robert Williams standing at the cashier. Turning, he spotted them. "Well, hello," he said affably.

Christina flushed at the sight of him. Robert took her in with a languorous sweep of his eyes, smiling. But it was Bill he addressed.

"Are you two golfers?"

"Let's say I'm trying to coax Chris into becoming a player," Bill said. "How about you?"

"I'm a hacker," Robert said. "I play with my brother-in-law two or three times a year, and that's about it." He glanced at Christina. "I felt like getting some exercise. Tennis is really my game, but it's hard to play tennis by yourself. So here I am, at the golf course."

"I'm a golf fanatic," Bill said, "but not very good. My handicap's around twenty. If tennis is your game, talk to Chris. She's fabulous. In fact, she's a hell of an athlete. Runs like a deer."

"Oh?" Robert said, glancing her way. "A lady of many hidden talents."

Christina gave him a withering look.

"I'd invite you to join us," Bill said, oblivious to the interplay between her and Robert, "but our tee time isn't for an hour."

"I'm due up in a few minutes," Robert said. "Why don't you join me? I can check with the pro to make sure it's all right."

"Gee, we wouldn't want to impose," Bill said, not in the least sounding like he meant it.

"No, we wouldn't," Christina chimed in, more emphatically.

"It's no imposition," Robert insisted. "I'm alone. I'd be less likely to cheat with you watching, Bill," he added, giving Christina a wink.

She could have slugged him. How could he be making private jokes with her, given the circumstances? And why was he trying to socialize with them? Had he no sense of propriety?

"Well, gee," Bill said, obviously liking the idea, "if Chris doesn't mind . . ."

Christina gave Bill a dark look, too. He'd heard what she'd said about her not wanting to have a drink with Robert Williams. How could he possibly think a round of golf with the man would be okay with her? But he'd put her on the spot and there was no graceful way out.

"Why would I mind?" she said unconvincingly.

Still, both Robert and Bill looked pleased. It was clear her feelings didn't matter to either one of them.

"I'll negotiate with the pro," Bill said. "Do you want to grab a cool drink before we go out on the course, Chris?"

"No, I don't need anything."

"I've rented a golf cart," Bill said to Robert. "Do you have one?"

"I was going to carry my clubs," Robert replied. "Frankly, the walking interests me more than hitting the ball."

"Not me. *Exercise* is a dirty word as far as I'm concerned. Chris'll tell you." Bill slapped him on the back in a friendly way. "Ride with us, Bob. We can squeeze three in the cart."

Christina rolled her eyes. She could have killed Bill. Robert, for his part, acted bemused, if not pleased. She was sure this was exactly what he wanted. Lord, the thought of being wedged between him and Bill in a golf cart for a couple of hours was enough to make her nauseous.

"Sweetheart, while I'm at the pro shop, show Bob where our cart is, will you?"

"Certainly."

Bill went off and she turned to Robert. "You're a real bastard, you know that," she said, trying to show her disgust.

"Why? Because I offered to share my tee time and save your fiancé an hour?"

"You know perfectly well what I mean, *Bob*."

"It's Robert. Only coffee moguls call me Bob."

"If you were a gentleman, you'd have bowed out, saved me the humiliation and embarrassment."

"It seems Bill is oblivious to our little misadventure, so what's the problem?"

"*You're* the problem! Can't you understand I don't want to see you, or be reminded of what happened?"

"Well, I'm sorry you feel that way," he said. "I've spent the morning savoring my memories, wishing that somehow we might have the opportunity to get to know each other . . . perhaps become friends."

"It's not going to happen," she snapped. "I'm committed to Bill. I'm going to marry him, so forget it. Forget me." She pointed toward the door. "I'll show you where the golf cart is, so you can load your golf bag."

They left for the clubhouse. Robert found his bag and slung it over his shoulder.

"What's Bill's great appeal, if you don't mind me asking? Is it his money?"

Christina gave him a dirty look. "No, it's not his money."

"Then what?"

"Bill is a very kind, very sweet person. He's generous, decent, funny, intelligent, upbeat. And he loves me."

"Interesting."

"What's interesting?"

"You had a whole long litany, and not once did you say that you loved him."

"Of course I love him."

"Of course?"

"It goes without saying. I wouldn't marry him if I didn't love him."

"Hmm," Robert said, pondering her comment. "How do you define love?"

"It's none of your business!"

They'd come to the golf cart. Robert put his bag alongside theirs. Christina looked off toward the pro shop, hoping to see Bill, but he wasn't in sight. She turned to Robert, crossing her arms as she glared at him through her sunglasses. He was smiling at her. Mr. Charm.

"Look, Robert, don't make the mistake of thinking that what happened last night means something. The lights were off, I was drunk. You could have been anyone. Literally."

"I know you don't love me . . ."

"Ha," she said, rolling her eyes as if to say, "No kidding."

". . . you don't know me, and I don't know you," he went on.

"And that's just where it's going to end," she interjected.

"Maybe. Probably. But don't you believe in . . . chemistry, fate, love at first sight, destiny? Things like that?"

"I believe in knowing someone, caring about them, relating to them and wanting to spend your life with them. That's what Bill and I share."

Robert stroked his chin. "You aren't even curious whether those good vibrations in the dark would also work in daylight, in other contexts?"

"Friction is not love."

"Granted. So, what is love to you?"

"It's what I feel for Bill."

"Stubborn little thing, aren't you?"

"Listen, Mr. Williams, my desire to be alone with the man I intend to marry does not make me stubborn. It's a blow to your ego, I know, but it happens to be the truth. Second, I'm not little. I'm five-nine and weigh a hundred and twenty-two pounds."

"And you're the most beautiful woman I've ever seen."

"Please."

"It's true. On my honor, Christina. My sacred honor."

"With all due respect, you need to get a life."

"I have one. But last evening I was seated in the garden, and when I looked up I saw an incredible goddess who was staring out to sea, her long hair blowing in the breeze. In my thirty-seven years I'd never seen such a lovely sight.

"Then later, in the bar, I saw her again. And it was love at first sight, Christina. Granted, I knew it wasn't real, that it was all in my head. But then you came to my bed, I made love to you—not only with my body, but with my soul. You were a dream come true. How can I not love you, or at least love the promise of what you might be?"

Christina was stunned by his speech. Moved by it, in spite of herself. But she knew she couldn't be taken in by it any more than she could be taken in by his prowess at lovemaking.

"I thought you were under the impression I was someone you'd met in the bar, someone who'd come on to you. You weren't making love to me any more than

I was making love to you, Robert, so how can you suddenly claim all these romantic feelings?"

"When you woke me up, my first thought was that it was Patsy. In the course of the night, the woman I was with somehow became you. At some level I knew, or wanted to believe, that you were the goddess I'd seen from the garden."

"That makes sleeping with me even worse," she said, looking again in the direction of the pro shop.

"I was with *you*, Christina. That's what matters."

She started getting nervous. "Well, I was with Bill."

"Forgive me for saying this, but I don't believe you. I don't believe you love that man the way you should if you're going to become his wife."

"Believe anything you want. I know who I love and who I'll marry. I'd be grateful if you'd let it drop. We're stuck with each other for a few hours, but that doesn't mean you can't respect my feelings. If you force this, I'll have no choice but to tell Bill what happened. So, my advice is to accept things as they are."

"You're right. I must respect your feelings. But I want you to know I appreciate you listening to me. And you're right about another thing. I may be deluding myself. What you don't understand is that you might be, too."

They both turned at the sound of Bill's voice. "Sorry it took so long," he said, approaching them, "but the pro was reluctant to move us up. I had to persuade him."

"Sounds like you found his weakness," Robert said.

"Yes, indeed," Bill said, grinning. "There's not a soul on earth who can't be had, if the price is right."

"Interesting philosophy, Bill," Robert said. "Tell me, do you think love has a price, as well?"

"What are we talking about, sex?"

"No, romantic love. Passion. Can that be bought?" He glanced at Christina, who glared at him through narrowed eyes.

"I think feelings have a way of adapting," Bill said. "Take the coffeehouse business. I was sure my passion was electronics till I came across a terrific business opportunity. Suddenly, I loved coffee. The smell of the stuff, anything and everything to do with coffee, appealed to me."

"That sounds like something a successful man would say," Robert said. "A guy's got to understand himself before he can make his mark. And you're right. For a lot of people, passion follows the dollar."

"That's certainly been my experience."

Robert turned to her. "How about you, Christina? What do you think?"

"I think we should play golf." With that, she turned and climbed into the golf cart.

"Now there's a woman who understands *my* passions," Bill said.

He got behind the wheel. Robert climbed in the other side. Christina was wedged between them. Their hips and thighs were all touching. She was very much aware of both men, but there was fire, and it was coming from the body of the man she'd slept with the night before. Her passion, or whatever it was, seemed to have a mind of its own. She hated Robert Williams for that, she truly did.

8

CHRISTINA AWOKE with a start. Someone was banging on the door. She sat up in a grip of panic, looking around to see if Robert was still there. But she was alone. True, Bill, in a rage, had been looking for Robert, but that was only in her dream. It hadn't actually happened.

There was another loud knock. She got up and opened the door. Bill stood there, his shirt soaked with perspiration. He looked limp.

"Did I wake you, sweetheart? Sorry, I forgot my key."

"That's all right," she said, rubbing her eyes. "What time is it, anyway?"

Bill patted her cheek as he stepped past her. "Almost two."

Christina closed the door. "I didn't mean to sleep so long. I guess I conked out."

"I'm glad you were still resting," he said, heading for the bath. "I was afraid you'd be starving and furious with me. Bob and I had a beer after we finished the round. The time got away from me. I'll just grab a quick shower and then we can go eat."

He closed the bathroom door, leaving Christina wondering. Evidently nothing catastrophic had oc-

curred after she'd dropped out of the golf game at the
ninth hole and returned to the hotel. She wasn't sure
what might happen with just the two of them, but she'd
felt too miserable to care. Between her hangover, the
sun and Robert's quips, winks and meaningful looks,
she hadn't been able to go on with the charade.

"You two can fight it out for the championship," she'd
told them as they passed the clubhouse at the midway
point of the round. "I'm getting off the bus."

"That's a hell of a note," Robert had said. "Now we'll
have nothing to look at but the view."

"Suffer," she'd replied, arching a brow. And she'd
meant it.

From the first hole, the men had fought each other
like a pair of tigers. After nine, Bill was up two strokes
but Robert was giving him a run for his money. The ri-
valry was bad enough, but what really got to her was
the way Robert behaved, especially after Bill took off
after a ball that had gone into the rough and she was
alone with Robert again.

"Suppose I could get Bill to play me for you?" he'd
asked. "After all, he said earlier that everyone has a
price. What do you think he'd want for you? A hundred thousand? A million?"

"I have no idea. You'd have to ask him."

"Well, I wouldn't put you up as a stake for any price,"
Robert said. "There are some things money can't buy,
your beloved fiancé's conviction to the contrary notwithstanding."

"Bill's not as mercenary as you think."

"Nothing in the world would keep him from marrying you?"

"Nothing he's ever mentioned."

"Why was your wedding called off, anyway?"

Christina hesitated. "Due to some complications in Bill's settlement negotiations with his wife."

"She wanted too much money to give him his divorce?"

"Well, it's a little more complicated than that," she said, realizing she'd fallen into a trap. "By delaying things a few months he stands to save millions."

"I see."

"Don't try to make something of that," she said. "You'd do the same. Besides, what difference does it make? We're serious about marrying. We didn't even postpone the honeymoon."

"Now that was an astute move on his part," Robert said. "I've always admired men who manage to have their cake and eat it, too."

"Oh, go to hell," she'd said, walking off and leaving him alone under his banyan tree.

She wasn't sure why Robert got under her skin. The man was arrogant and smug. What he hoped to accomplish by putting Bill down, she didn't know. It certainly didn't make her think any more of him.

She could hear Bill singing in the shower. He didn't have a bad voice, but it irritated her anyway. She hadn't realized that until now. In fact, all morning she'd been somewhat miffed at him for playing into Robert's trap.

Why didn't Bill see that Robert was mentally undressing her with every leering glance?

Hearing the shower stop, she knew she had to get dressed. She went to the closet, delighted that their luggage had come so that she could wear her yellow cotton T-shirt dress. The skirt was short and the sleeveless dress had a scoop neck and low back. She was smoothing it over her hips when the bathroom door opened. Bill appeared in a cloud of steam, a towel wrapped around his middle.

"So, who won the golf match?" she asked.

"I did," Bill said with a grin. "Beat him by four strokes." He applied deodorant. "Which means *he* owes *us* dinner."

"You mean we're going to have to spend the evening with him, too?" she groused, ready to kill him.

"No, sweetheart, I told him you'd probably want a quiet room service meal tonight. We'll have the payoff dinner in Seattle."

"How could you, Bill? You know I don't like the man."

He turned, regarding her with surprise. "You didn't say anything about not liking him. You said you wanted us to be alone on our honeymoon. That's all."

"Well, it's the same thing," she said.

"No, it isn't. What don't you like about the guy?"

"He's arrogant. And glib. And smug."

Bill wiped the steam off the bathroom mirror so he could comb his hair. "You think so?"

"Well, it's just an opinion. If you want to have dinner with him, feel free. But leave me out of it."

"I'd have thought that him being a writer and in public television, you'd have liked him, or at least found him interesting."

He removed the towel from around his waist and tossed it aside. Christina looked at his naked body. She remembered her glimpse of Robert in the buff. There was no comparison. Robert was Adonis beside Bill. It annoyed her that it was true, and it annoyed her even more that she cared.

Bill came into the bedroom to get fresh underwear. She went to the sliding glass doors overlooking the deck and looked out.

"Bob suggested a rematch," Bill said. "Tennis this time. Said he'd scrounge up a doubles partner and they'd take us on. We have a tentative date with him in the morning."

Christina sighed with exasperation. How could Bill allow himself to be manipulated this way? If she just told him what had happened, that would put an end to it. There'd be no more socializing with Robert Williams, that's for sure. "Wonderful," she said dryly. "Can't think of anything I'd rather do."

"Hey," Bill said, "if you don't want to, we'll skip it."

She turned to face him. "I don't mean to be a spoilsport, but I don't want to socialize with the man."

"Hey, if Bob's a problem, no sweat."

"Robert. His name is Robert. He doesn't like to be called Bob."

Bill blinked with surprise. "Oh. If you say so."

She shrugged. "He . . . mentioned that this morning."

"Look," Bill said, "I'll cancel."

"No, I'll do whatever you want."

Bill put his hands on his hips, frustrated. "Give me some help, Chris. Do you want me to get rid of him or not?"

"I don't care whether we socialize with him or not. Just so long as you don't invite him to sleep with us."

Bill laughed. "I'm not prepared to go quite that far."

Christina blushed and turned back to the window. "Thank God for small favors," she mumbled.

Bill came over and, standing behind her, wrapped his arms around her. He kissed her hair. "All I want is for you to be happy, sweetheart. You know that, don't you?"

She nodded, doing her best to act positive, but tears welled in her eyes anyway. She was glad Bill didn't notice because it would have been difficult for her to explain why they were there.

"So, are you getting hungry?" he asked.

"Yes, actually, I am."

"Then let's go have us something to eat. Just you and me."

THE RESTAURANT was open-sided and overlooked the garden and pool. They had a table right at the edge, commanding a wonderful view of the grounds and the sea beyond. For the first time that day Christina actually felt human. The nap had done wonders. Her stomach seemed in condition to accept food, though she didn't want anything too rich.

Bill, his nose a bit burned from the sun, leaned back in his chair and looked out at the guests frolicking by the pool. Some were swimming, others were sunning themselves in lounge chairs. He inhaled the warm, fragrant air drifting in the open building. "Ah, this is the life, eh, Chris? A morning of golf. Lunch with the woman I love. Maybe a snooze this afternoon, and an evening of . . . what? Merriment?"

Christina couldn't help but smile at him. At times Bill Roberts seemed more like an adolescent boy than a man of nearly forty. He had a devil-may-care innocence that could be very appealing. Yet at the same time he could be a focused, hard-nosed businessman. She knew that because she'd gone to a business dinner with him once where he ended up negotiating a deal with a hard-driving adversary. Bill was no cream puff.

She sometimes wondered what it was about him she treasured most. He was upbeat, amusing, good-natured. And optimistic. The day she'd met him, she knew Bill had the world by the tail. It had been at a banquet for the various businesses, foundations and organizations that underwrote the station's programming. The staff's job was to charm, humor and entertain their benefactors, as appropriate. She'd sat next to Bill, and he'd glommed on to her at once, convincing her into going out with him for a drink afterward. Before they'd said good-night, Bill had informed her that he intended to marry her.

He and Kelly were already separated at the time, but even so, Christina hadn't taken him seriously. She'd taken the comment as an extension of his bantering style, his general affability. But it soon became clear he was serious. Dead serious.

Bill showered her with gifts and attention like no man she'd ever known. It was pretty obvious he was crazy about her. She'd never felt so wanted before. Bill Roberts had moved in on her with the zeal of a corporate raider, hell-bent on having her, whatever the price.

For the first month or two she humored herself, allowing him to show her a good time. She'd never gone out with a man who had serious money before, and probably allowed herself to be dazzled. Bill was a master at courting, at making her feel valued. Things between them became serious almost without her being aware of what had happened. The life he'd painted for her as the future Mrs. William Roberts was seductive. She'd have her career, as much freedom as she wanted. All that was really required of her was that she be his consort, share his life and riches.

Christina had never thought of herself as mercenary. She could honestly say she hadn't accepted his offer of marriage for the money, though in fairness she'd have to admit his life-style was a major part of the package he offered. She liked Bill and there was something to be said for a man who made a woman feel very, very special — which Bill did to perfection.

The waiter came. Bill opted for a beer and Christina a mineral water while they looked over the menus.

"So, what would you say, Chris? Are you ninety percent recovered from your night of debauchery?"

She assumed he was referring to the excess of Mai Tais—a recovery that would come more quickly than the recovery from the debauchery he knew nothing about. "More like fifty or sixty," she replied.

"I know how it can be. Once in college I got dead drunk and was sick for three days."

"I certainly hope it won't take me that long." She smiled at him. "I took two more aspirin, so that may help."

"Maybe all you need is a bit of romance," he said, twitching his brows.

"Is it really romance you mean, Bill?"

He grinned. Then, leaning across the table, he said in a low voice, "Need I remind you this marriage has yet to be consummated?"

She leaned toward him and replied in the same tone, "Need I remind you that the real Mrs. William Roberts is in California, not sitting across the table from you?"

The corner of his mouth twitched. "You're getting technical on me."

"I'm just reminding you it isn't a marriage, yet."

"But it is a honeymoon," he said, looking defensive.

She furrowed her brow in sympathy. "Poor Bill. Do you feel deprived?"

"I know there's a theory that keeping 'em wanting is a sure way of keeping 'em interested, but, sweetheart, you don't need to play hard to get. I'm yours for the taking."

She chuckled. "I'll keep that in mind, Bill."

The waiter returned with their drinks. Christina took a deep breath of the balmy air drifting in from the garden. She wasn't about to tell Bill, but she had been thinking about sex a lot that day. Unfortunately it wasn't about sex with him—at least not in a positive sense. She'd thought about Robert almost incessantly, the way it had been last night.

Christina felt bad about that. Yet oddly, as the day had worn on, she'd felt increasingly less guilty toward Bill and more resentful. She didn't like the way he'd allowed Robert to impose on them so often. The man was competing with Bill for her heart, and her fiancé didn't even realize what was going on.

But even worse, she didn't like it that Bill was rapidly losing his appeal. He seemed to pale in comparison with Robert. It wasn't as if he was repulsive or anything, but she had lost her desire to be with him, and to make love with him. Two days earlier she wanted more than anything to marry him, and now she found herself plotting strategies for avoiding his bed.

Why? That was the question that haunted her. Was it her tumble in the hay with Robert? Could a night of great sex with someone else change her feelings toward a man she'd promised to marry? Christina hated to think she could be that fickle, that superficial.

Passion. That was the word that kept coming to her mind. She'd felt lots of things for Bill, lots of good things. But never passion. And maybe she'd never felt it for anyone else, either. But last night, for several sterling hours, she'd been enraptured, blissful, imbued with what seemed like passion.

It was Robert Williams, yes. But was it also the Mai Tais, the massage, the tropical night? Had the whole thing been a magical accident of chemistry? A one-shot deal, in other words? Was she being a fool to let it upset her life, the future she'd given careful and considerate thought to? Most telling was the fact that she hadn't been able to put the incident from her mind. She certainly wasn't the only woman who loved one man and—for whatever reason—ended up sleeping with another. In such circumstances, didn't love triumph in the end? Shouldn't she be able to forget Robert Williams and return to her life? Of course she should! So why was she having such a hard time?

"By golly," Bill said, "I think we've solved the mystery of the phantom woman."

Christina saw that he was staring down at the pool. She turned to see what he was looking at. "What do you mean?"

"Bob's—I mean, Robert's—lady friend from last night. See her down there by the pool, the babe in the hot pink bikini?"

Christina searched the rows of lounge chairs. She didn't have to look for long. The "babe in the hot pink bikini" was at the near end. She was a short, curvy blonde with hair piled up on her head. She was wearing one of those tiny string bikinis that consisted of

three minuscule patches of fabric. When she turned her
back to them, she might as well have been naked.

Christina could see why Bill had made the associa-
tion with Robert. The blonde was talking to a good-
looking guy with a body of his own. He was in skimpy
black racing trunks and his broad, furry chest was
every bit as impressive as the blonde's full, ripe breasts.
It was Robert Williams himself.

"Quite a pair, eh?" Bill said, evidently sharing the
same thought as she.

"Yes," Christina said vacantly, her eyes glued on the
couple, "I guess so."

"Lord," Bill said, shaking his head in awe.

She did not like the worshipful tone and gave him a
look. "What makes you think they were together last
night?"

Bill shrugged. "Boy talk this morning when we were
playing the back nine."

"What did Robert say?" Christina asked, her curiosity very much aroused.

"Ah, nothing really."

"Bill, that's really frustrating—to start a story and
quit in the middle."

"Well, I just asked him if he was responsible for the
symphony of pleasure ringing through the neighbor-
hood last night."

Christina flushed, her cheeks turning to fire. "And
he said . . ."

"He was modest. Said he hoped it didn't disturb my
sleep."

She groaned and looked back down at the pool. Robert had gotten to his feet and was engaged in an animated conversation with the blonde. To Christina's amazement, a flash of jealousy went through her.

"So, what makes you think that's the woman?" she asked.

"I'm speculating." For a few seconds he watched the poolside flirtation. "I'd say there's some chemistry there, wouldn't you?"

As they watched, Robert went with the blonde to where she'd been sunning herself. He picked up her lounge chair and carried it back next to his spot, then set it down.

"He's obviously a womanizer," she said with a touch more hostility than she wanted.

"He's the type women go for, let's put it that way."

"There's no one type, Bill. Women have varying tastes in men."

"So, how do you find him? Just another pretty face?"

"I try not to ogle other men. Not on my honeymoon."

Bill turned back to her. "I wasn't ogling Robert's little blond friend. I was just curious about her."

"Don't apologize. Men are supposed to look at women. Especially if they're dressed like that. There'd be something wrong with you if you didn't."

Bill chuckled. "Then it's all right if I hope Blondie is Robert's doubles partner tomorrow?"

Christina was about to ask if he really intended to keep the tennis date, when she decided to heck with it.

A little tennis might even be fun. "Let's hope for Robert's sake and your sake that she is."

Bill gave his trademark good-natured laugh. "Might be hard for me to keep my eye on the bouncing ball if she shows up."

She glanced at the pool again. Robert was stretched out on his stomach and the bimbo was bending over him, her fanny pointed in their direction, putting suntan lotion on his back.

"Don't worry, Bill, I'll keep us in the game."

Her fiancé seemed not to hear. "You think Robert'll treat us to another nocturnal performance tonight?" he asked absently.

"Would you like that?" Christina asked.

He gave her a bemused look. "Would you?"

9

CHRISTINA LAY in the dark, listening to the sound of the surf coming through the open sliding doors. The lulling rhythm was punctuated by Bill's sputtering snore. She was relieved he had fallen asleep quickly. Her only regret was that she hadn't, as well.

Things had been uncomfortable when they'd gone to bed because she hadn't wanted to make love. She'd claimed she still felt crummy, and Bill hadn't questioned her. But at some level he had to know she just wasn't interested. That wasn't an easy thing to take, not while on one's honeymoon.

To make matters worse, even though she was in bed with Bill, Christina's mind had been on Robert during most of the past hour. For some reason she was really annoyed by the way he had cavorted with that bimbo down at the pool. Not that Christina was jealous—it was more a kind of resentment for having thereby cheapened their time together. The woman in his bed last night—the one who'd shared those hours of glorious sex—could just as easily have been the bosomy blonde as her. She'd just happened to walk in the door first. Christina was willing to bet that Miss String Bikini was next door right now, having her strings ceremoniously untied.

Of course, it didn't matter. Robert meant nothing to her. How could she care about someone she'd known for less than a day? She looked at the luminous dial on her travel clock. It was past eleven—exactly twenty-four hours since she'd crawled into Robert's bed. Christina shivered at the thought.

She turned to look at the moonlight coming in the sliding glass doors. It was a lovely night—hardly one to spend tossing and turning, feeling frustrated and resentful. She got up, went over to the sliding door and looked at the sparkling surf. The air was so inviting she decided to go out on the deck.

Fumbling in the dark, she found her T-shirt that she'd stripped off once Bill was asleep. She put it on and stepped onto the deck. A soft breeze greeted her. It felt heavenly.

Christina glanced toward bungalow twelve and was surprised to see a faint glow of light spilling onto the deck from inside. Was Robert up? Was he alone?

She stood at the railing, listening to the wind in the palm trees, the muted roar of the surf and the ominous silence coming from next door. What did it mean? Maybe Blondie wasn't a screamer, and that was why it was so quiet.

Christina colored at the notion. Lord. She hadn't thought of herself as a screamer, either, until Bill had made such a big deal about it. So far as she knew, she'd never done that before.

NO COST! NO OBLIGATION TO BUY! NO PURCHASE NECESSARY!

PLAY "LUCKY 7" AND GET FIVE FREE GIFTS

HOW TO PLAY:

1. With a coin, carefully scratch off the silver box at the right. Then check the claim chart to see what we have for you—FREE BOOKS and a gift—ALL YOURS! ALL FREE!

2. Send back this card and you'll receive brand-new Harlequin Temptation® novels. These books have a cover price of $3.50 each, but they are yours to keep absolutely free.

3. There's no catch. You're under no obligation to buy anything. We charge nothing—ZERO—for your first shipment. And you don't have to make any minimum number of purchases—not even one!

4. The fact is thousands of readers enjoy receiving books by mail from the Harlequin Reader Service®. They like the convenience of home delivery . . . they like getting the best new novels before they're available in stores . . . and they love our discount prices!

5. We hope that after receiving your free books you'll want to remain a subscriber. But the choice is yours—to continue or cancel, anytime at all! So why not take us up on our invitation, with no risk of any kind. You'll be glad you did!

YOURS FREE!

*This beautiful porcelain box is topped with a lovely bouquet of porcelain flowers, perfect for holding rings, pins or other precious trinkets — and is yours **absolutely free** when you accept our no risk offer!*

PLAY "LUCKY 7"

**Just scratch off the silver box with a coin.
Then check below to see the gifts you get.**

YES! I have scratched off the silver box. Please send me all the gifts for which I qualify. I understand I am under no obligation to purchase any books, as explained on the back and on the opposite page.

142 CIH AZJV
(U-H-T-05/96)

NAME

ADDRESS   APT.

CITY   STATE   ZIP

 WORTH FOUR FREE BOOKS PLUS A FREE TRINKET BOX

 WORTH THREE FREE BOOKS

 WORTH TWO FREE BOOKS

WORTH ONE FREE BOOK

THE HARLEQUIN READER SERVICE®: HERE'S HOW IT WORKS

Accepting free books places you under no obligation to buy anything. You may keep the books and gift and return the shipping statement marked "cancel". If you do not cancel, about a month later we'll send you 4 additional novels, and bill you just $2.66 each plus 25¢ delivery and applicable sales tax, if any.* That's the complete price, and—compared to cover prices of $3.50 each—quite a bargain! You may cancel at any time, but if you choose to continue, every month we'll send you 4 more books, which you may either purchase at the discount price...or return at our expense and cancel your subscription.

*Terms and prices subject to change without notice. Sales tax applicable in N.Y.

BUSINESS REPLY MAIL
FIRST-CLASS MAIL   PERMIT NO. 717   BUFFALO, NY

POSTAGE WILL BE PAID BY ADDRESSEE

HARLEQUIN READER SERVICE
3010 WALDEN AVE
PO BOX 1867
BUFFALO NY 14240-9952

NO POSTAGE
NECESSARY
IF MAILED
IN THE
UNITED STATES

She kept looking at Robert's bungalow, her curiosity getting the best of her. Maybe if she were a little closer she'd be able to hear if anything was going on.

The next thing she knew, she was creeping across the sand between the two bungalows. Drawing closer, she saw that Robert's sliding door was open. But there was no sound coming from inside. Maybe they were resting between sessions, or asleep.

Reaching the base of the steps, Christina listened, her eyes closed, as she tried to catch a sigh, a moan.

"Go on up if you like," came a voice from behind her.

She let out a startled cry. Spinning, she searched the shadows, but didn't see him at first. Then she made out the lines of a hammock strung between two palm trees. Robert was in it, stretched out with his hands behind his head. She could see the white of his shorts and the white of his teeth. She was sure he was smiling, though she couldn't see his face.

"Dear God, you scared me to death," she gasped.

Robert sat up, resting his bare feet in the sand. "I didn't mean to. It looked like you were about to pay me a friendly visit, so I was just trying to be hospitable."

"I was not paying you a visit," she snapped. "Friendly or otherwise."

He moved toward her with graceful strides. Christina felt her stomach tighten. Her instinct was to run, but that would look dumb. Anyway, she hadn't the strength to move.

Robert stopped before her, his face now plainly visible in the moonlight, his furry chest and broad shoulders a monument of masculinity. "Then you must be out for a walk," he said, masking the sarcasm that was surely in his thoughts.

"Yes, as a matter of fact, I was," she replied, knowing she had no better explanation.

Robert seemed totally unconcerned that he was in his underwear, whereas she was painfully conscious of the fact that all that stood between her and nakedness were her T-shirt and panties. Christina was certain her nipples were poking through the thin cotton shirt. Again, she had to fight the urge to run away.

"Perhaps you'd like to stop and rest a spell," he said. "Walking in the sand can be so tiring."

"Very funny, *Bob*."

"Touché."

"You're really not a very nice person, you know," she said, finding her courage. "All that flirting this morning on the golf course...and the double entendres...were just to make a joke at Bill's expense."

"The last thing in the world I'd do is make a joke of last night," he said firmly, "even at Bill's expense. Besides which, I've already told you how I feel about making love with you."

"Please. I didn't come here for more of your bull."

"Then why did you come?" He glanced down at her bare legs.

Christina glared at him. Unfortunately, there was nothing in her mind but the truth. "Since you're so determined to hear me say it, I'll tell you. I was curious who you were with tonight." Her eyes flashed. "There.

Does that make you feel better? Did your ego get a boost?"

"And what makes you so sure I'd be with someone?"

Christina peered into his eyes. They were dark and brooding. "Because sometimes lightning does strike twice in the same place. Last night was me. Tonight another drunk might have stumbled into your bed."

"And did you have any candidate in mind for this evening's romp?" he asked lightly. She shrugged and looked away.

"Did you?"

She hated his persistence. "Okay, the blonde in the hot pink bikini. There, are you satisfied, Mr. Williams?"

Robert laughed. She gave him another evil stare.

"How do you know about Patsy?" he asked.

"God knows, it would've been hard to miss her. That was quite a performance . . . the way she was slathering suntan lotion all over your back."

Robert laughed, sounding almost delighted. "You're jealous."

"I most certainly am not!"

"Then why . . ."

"I'm simply explaining why it was perfectly reasonable to assume you had a woman with you. Miss Tonight."

"As opposed to Miss Last Night?"

She shook her head with disgust. "Don't gloat. It's not becoming."

"Forgive me. What I meant to say is, you wanted to know if last night was a routine occurrence, another day at the office, so to speak."

"Yes, I was curious. I'll admit that. I couldn't sleep. I stepped out onto the deck, saw the light and wondered, 'Now is it the blonde at the pool, or has ol' Robert snared someone else this evening?' So I sneaked over for a little peek and you caught me. Satisfied?"

He looked at her a long time, then quietly said, "Is that what you really think of me? That I'm a womanizer?"

There was genuine hurt in his voice. Christina was almost sure he wasn't acting. Her first instinct was to reassure him, to tell him that she didn't mean to hurt him, but she was afraid of the way that sounded. Besides, the last thing she wanted was to give him the wrong impression. So she said nothing.

"I've never had to struggle to find a girl to take to the dance," he said when she didn't answer him. "I grant you that. But I'm not a Casanova, either. Things have changed for me the last year or so, mainly because of this PBS series I did. When a person recognizes you, or hears you've been on television, they want to touch you. But it doesn't mean anything."

"And what happened between us did? Is that what you're implying?"

"You just won't give me the benefit of the doubt, will you?" he said sadly.

"With all due respect, I don't think I owe you anything."

"Maybe you don't...unless it's honesty." He sighed, running his hand back through his hair. "I know you think I'm a romantic fool, but I feel in my gut that something unique happened between us and I can't let go of it. Can you honestly tell me you didn't feel it, too?"

"I won't drop Bill to pursue a fantasy," she said. "Even if you're right and there was more to last night than just sex, the sad truth is that you don't know me. Not the real me."

"But I want to know you."

"Well, I don't want—" She stopped midsentence. For some reason she couldn't say it.

He took her other hand and pulled her closer. "You don't want *me*? Is that what you're trying to say?"

"I don't want you messing up my life. Don't you see, you're being completely unrealistic. You can call it fate or destiny—any damned thing you want—but to me what's happened between us is just plain crazy."

He lightly stroked her cheek with the back of his finger. His eyes glistened. His expression was almost worshipful. "I'm tempted to say, 'Come inside with me and I'll show you how wrong you are.' But I won't." He stared down at the sand, obviously considering how to say what was in his mind. "What harm would it do to put your engagement on hold for a while? In a couple of weeks I'll be in Seattle. Go out with me. Get to know me."

"I can't."

"Why not?"

"Because it's insane," she said. "You may not see that, but I do." She turned to walk away, but Robert made her face him again. She started to protest, but before a sound could pass her lips, his mouth covered hers. The kiss was forceful, dominating, almost angry. She tried to wrench free, but he was practically inhaling her.

Then, after a second or two, a powerful, over-whelming desire came over her and the next thing she knew she was kissing him as hard as he kissed her. The fire of the night before was there. Only this time there was no pretense, no illusion about it being Bill. This was Robert Williams in the flesh, and she wanted him desperately, irrationally, insanely.

He'd lifted her into his arms even before their lips parted. As he carried her up the steps, she took his face in her hands and kissed him harder than before.

It could have been fire she was breathing. Her nostrils flared, and so did his. Her teeth clenched, his jaw drew taut. He tossed her onto the bed. Then he shoved the sliding glass door shut with a finality that under-scored his determination.

Christina rose to her knees and whipped off her T-shirt, tossing it aside as he moved toward her. It was as if they'd said simultaneously, "Damn it, let's do it and get it over with."

He took off his shorts and she her panties. In the passing of an instant they were in each other's arms. He landed on her with a thud. She rolled over on top of him, pushing herself up so that she was astride him. She looked into his eyes. There was no playful smile on his face, no look of bemusement, no chiding scowl—just hunger. And determination.

Christina leaned on his chest, digging her fingers into his mat of hair, defying him to take her. Reaching up, he pulled her face down to his and kissed her again.

A hot river ran through her. There was nothing to wait for. This was sex, pure and simple, and they both knew it. She wanted him to take her and be done with it.

Robert didn't have to be asked. He had her on her back instantly, her legs apart. She cried out when he entered her. She dug her nails into his back and bit his lip. Then, as he thrust into her, she turned her head away, listening to her own cries of pleasure, not caring who heard, just wanting to have her orgasm and him to have his, so it would be over with.

Their bodies were heaving in unison when they came. She outlasted him, undulating long after he was spent. The pulsing continued for several minutes and she savored the sensation, knowing it was finite, if eternal. She was only moments from becoming herself again.

Robert seemed to sense he was about to lose her— that in taking her, he'd truly lost her. They were both soaked with sweat. He kissed her wet hair, her neck. She could tell there were things he wanted to say, but dared not. It was just as well. They wouldn't have mattered.

Christina wedged her hand under his shoulder and pushed him off. Then she sat up on the edge of the bed, feeling practically as dizzy as she had the night before.

She found her panties and put them on. She turned her T-shirt right side out, then slipped it on, as well.

She glanced at Robert, who watched her with dark, sad eyes. His skin glistened, even through the mat of hair on his chest. The shadows from the lamplight molded his arms and thighs, even his sex. He'd won, but he'd also lost. She was walking away a free woman and he knew it.

At the sliding glass doors, Christina looked back at him a final time. He had the dignity not to speak, just as she had the strength to leave. Some battles had clear victors, others did not. Robert was doing his best to salvage what he could. She had to give him credit for that.

10

ROBERT OPTED to take a taxi from the television station to his hotel even though it was only seven blocks away. He didn't like walking in the rain, and Portland, he'd found to his chagrin, was even wetter than San Francisco. The day before his plane had landed at Portland International in a downpour, and he'd seen nothing but rain since. The only respite had come when he'd gone to dinner the previous evening. It was only drizzling then.

"Welcome to the real world, Robert," he said to himself as his plane touched down in Oregon, and it had been his mantra ever since. It wasn't that the mainland was depressing, but after a few days in paradise, favorable comparisons were hard to come by. Of course, his stay in Maui had ended on a down note, but that didn't detract from the blissful moments he'd enjoyed. But the sad fact was, the good Lord had probably given him his lifetime quota of good fortune in one fell swoop—at least when it came to romance.

Christina Cavanaugh, he knew with absolute certainty, was a once-in-a-lifetime experience. And her unceremonious departure from the Coral Reef had hurt him more than he could possibly say. It gave new meaning to the expression *a stake in the heart*.

"Here you are, sir," the driver said as they pulled up to the curb in front of the hotel.

Robert handed the man a ten-dollar bill. "Thanks."

"Stay dry."

Robert smiled weakly. It was probably what they said in the Pacific Northwest as an expression of greeting and farewell—a sort of maritime equivalent of "Aloha."

He didn't get too wet dashing to the door. The desk clerk cheerfully handed him his key, but refrained from saying, "Stay dry."

Thankfully, a dry elevator was waiting. It took him to his floor. "Stay dry," he muttered as he stepped out of the car, then, "Welcome to the real world." A maid who happened to be passing in the hall gave him a quizzical look.

"It's a long story," Robert said, glancing back at her.

She obviously didn't know what to make of him, imagining, probably, that he was nutty—another businessman who'd been in four towns in three days and wasn't sure where he was at the moment.

Robert trudged on down the hallway. The nutty part was about half-right, he decided. People in love behaved strangely. And Robert Williams was in misery. He had an excuse.

Robert managed to let himself into the right room, tossed his briefcase on a chair, took off his coat and plopped down on the bed without bothering to remove his shoes. He plucked the TV remote from the nightstand and turned on what he hoped would be the news. Instead he got a tennis match.

"Oh, swell."

For a moment he watched a girl in a short white skirt and long tanned legs taking ground strokes from the baseline. Two days ago he was to have met a long-legged, incomparably exquisite Christina Cavanaugh on the court and they were to have dueled to the death, using powerful forehands, withering glares, crisp backhands, come-hither or go-yonder looks—whatever and however. But it never happened.

Patsy had shown up at the appointed hour, racket in hand. As luck would have it, her girlfriend had hit it off with some guy who was with a convention and so the two women had extended their trip another day, though they'd had to change hotels. Patsy had let him know in no uncertain terms that she was happy with the change of schedule.

She was wearing the shortest, tightest tennis outfit he'd ever seen. "So where are our opponents?" she'd asked, turning to and fro to make sure he got a good look at her wares.

"I don't know," Robert said, sensing a bad omen.

He and bouncy Patsy had volleyed while they waited. Half an hour passed before a bellhop in an Aloha shirt came with a note from Bill. "Robert," the note had said, "Chris and I have had to return to the mainland. Sorry to stand you up like this, but it was unavoidable. Give me a call when you get to Seattle.

Dinner on you wouldn't be fair, since I denied you a re-match. I owe you a drink for reneging. Bill."

Bill Roberts's cryptic note had solved the mystery of why no tennis match, but it had, at the same time, created another, more perplexing mystery—why the sudden and unexpected end to the honeymoon? Robert was completely in the dark. They had left him high and dry. And wondering.

Maybe Christina had decided that throwing him into a state of confusion was the best revenge. For the past few days Robert had cursed himself for his weakness that last night, for giving in to desire, for playing the hare instead of the tortoise. It was no excuse that she'd wanted his body as much as he wanted hers. A woman's sexuality was sometimes a defensive weapon. It had been incumbent on him to prove that what he truly wanted was something much more profound than just sex. And he had failed.

The androgynous young woman on the television screen looked nothing like Christina, but she conveyed her spirit, striking the ball with fierceness and authority. It would have been that way between him and Christina on the tennis court, Bill and Patsy notwithstanding. Theirs would have been a secret dance of thrust and parry, overhead slam and ace. "Play with me, Christina," he would've challenged. "I'll think about it," she'd have replied. All without words—with only the tilt of a brow or the flip of a tennis skirt.

Robert pried his shoes off with his toes and let them drop to the floor beside the bed. *What of Seattle?* he asked himself, as the ball on the TV screen went ping, ping, ping and ping. Was there any hope for him?

It didn't matter whether she hated him or not—all that truly mattered was if he had failed her. That, he'd discovered over the years, was what mattered most to a woman. Validation. Did a man validate a woman's sense of self-worth, her femininity, her pride, her sexuality, her virtue, her passions? If he did, then he had her. Point, game, set, match, tournament. Till death do us part.

Bill, he surmised, was still sitting in the driver's seat. But Bill was married to someone else, and was over a barrel for the moment—a barrel filled with dollars. That was Robert's final glimmer of hope, his ace in the hole. But how did he exploit it? That was the question.

A woman's fidelity could be her most sacred possession. Convincing her it was misplaced without looking like a shark was one of the greatest challenges a man could face. It was an age-old problem with no easy solution. Far easier to come riding in on a white horse, swoop her off her feet and carry her into the night. That was a man's solution to a man's problem. Unfortunately he'd resorted to that with nothing to show for it but fifteen or twenty minutes of bliss and a boatload of regret.

THEY MOVED ALONG the bike path at a steady pace, she jogging, he on a trail bike pedaling beside her. The mist hung over Lake Washington, obscuring the far shore. Christina glanced out at the vista, noticing for the first

time three rowing shells skimming the gray-green water, pursued by a coaching launch. It was undoubtedly
one of the university crews, getting in an early-morning
workout.

She'd often wondered if rowing was something she'd
enjoy. The girls who did it competitively were tall, but
also strong. Christina had grit, but not a lot of strength.
Running suited her because of the freedom.

They were going slightly uphill now and Bill began
panting. She didn't slow down, knowing he could catch
her on the downhill stretches. Actually, she'd been a bit
annoyed when she'd come out of her building to find
him waiting for her with a brand-new bike and brand-
new sweats, an uninvited companion, raring to go.

"Figured I could keep up with you on a bike. Hope
you don't mind." That was all he said.

Christina had done a few stretches while he sat
astride the bike, staring at her bare legs. She'd said
nothing, her silence being her assent.

"You angry at me, Chris?" he'd asked as they headed
up the sidewalk toward the lake.

"No. Why do you ask?"

"You haven't been very friendly. I might as well be
blunt."

"Wanting a little space for a few days is not being un-
friendly."

"I'm feeling rejected."

"That isn't my intent, Bill."

At that point she'd picked up the pace, crossing the
street. Bill, who obviously hadn't done much biking,

had to concentrate on what he was doing. They'd been at it for fifteen minutes now without another word being said. Reaching the crest of a little hill, they started down and Bill was able to coast. He took a few deep breaths.

"So, if you aren't rejecting me, what *are* you doing?"

"Nothing."

"Come on, sweetheart, don't stonewall. Talk to me."

"I don't want you to get the wrong idea," she replied. "It's really no big deal."

"Try me."

Christina eased her pace, taking some deep breaths so she could talk and run at the same time. "It was a mistake going on a honeymoon when we weren't married."

"We had some bad luck, but I wouldn't call it a disaster."

"It was a disaster, Bill."

The path dropped off more steeply and he had to brake. "If we'd stayed, things would have smoothed out."

"Maybe. But I wasn't enjoying myself the way I wanted to, and you had a business crisis back here that needed tending to."

"*Why* weren't you enjoying yourself?" he asked. "That seems to be the issue."

The path started up again. Christina slowed even more.

"It's not you, Bill."

"You want to cut short your honeymoon and you're saying it's not me? Give me a break, Chris."

"It's not!"

"All right," he said, his exasperation beginning to show, "so it's not me. We took the wrong airline, used the wrong car rental company and stayed in the wrong hotel. Maybe Hawaii was a bad idea. Or maybe going on a honeymoon before the wedding was a bad idea. I take responsibility. But we're home now. Why aren't things different?"

Bill had fallen behind because he'd been talking instead of breathing. The path got steeper again so Christina slowed down to accommodate him. Bill got off his bike and walked beside her, breathing heavily.

"It's really, truly, not you," she said. "I'm just in a funky mood."

"Why?"

"I'm not sure. I just am." It was her first real lie. But how could she tell him the truth? She couldn't.

"It's us, isn't it? You have doubts about us. I made you go to Hawaii, it was miserable, and now you aren't sure you want to marry me."

"Don't be silly, Bill."

"That's what the evidence points to."

"You're making assumptions."

"I'm making assumptions because you won't talk to me."

She stopped in her tracks, putting her hands on her hips. "If you don't stop hounding me, you *will* be the problem. Can't you see that you're the victim in this as much as I am? If you want to blame anything, blame those damned Mai Tais I had."

"Chris, a good relationship should be able to survive a hangover, even a hangover on the honeymoon from hell."

"It will survive, if you'll just let me have some time alone."

"Sweetheart," he said, his voice pleading, "I'm just trying to get things on track, figure out what's happening to us."

Her eyes filled with tears as she looked up at him. She felt awful. Sick to her stomach with guilt. When she'd seen Bill waiting for her that morning with an expectant smile on his face, she'd actually felt nauseous. And it wasn't like her to be like that just because she was upset. But the nausea had passed as quickly as it had come.

Maybe the Hawaiian fiasco had affected her more profoundly than she'd realized. Getting in the wrong bed on her honeymoon hadn't just been a mistake, it might have changed her life forever. And even though she'd left Robert behind in Hawaii, she couldn't seem to get him out of her head, no matter how hard she tried.

Even that morning, when she was in that dreamy state between sleep and consciousness, she'd replayed their last time together in her mind. Their lovemaking had been so elemental. Almost as if Robert had stamped her with some invisible indelible mark.

Christina took a deep breath and looked at Bill. He was staring off across the lake. She could tell he was frustrated. She could hardly blame him.

"All right," he said, apparently tired of waiting for her to respond, "let's approach this differently. Tell me what you want from me. It's in your hands, Chris. You're the boss."

"I know I must seem like a spoiled brat."

"No, we won't play the blame game. That's not the issue. We're being very practical. Call it a problem-solving exercise."

She looked into his eyes. "You're a saint, Bill. You know that, don't you?"

"There are things I'd rather be, but thanks anyway."

She laughed, putting her hand on his arm affectionately. Bill Roberts was a decent man, a very decent man. She knew why she had wanted to marry him. In the absence of passionate love, he'd made perfect sense. But Hawaii had given her an experience she'd never had before—a taste of something else.

Splendor.

What she didn't know was how important that something else, that splendor, was. It could turn out that it wasn't important at all. It could turn out that her reason for having wanted to marry Bill in the first place was still valid.

She was looking down at her hands, thinking. He lifted her chin and made her look at him.

"All right, princess, what's it going to be? You get to set the rules of engagement."

"Give me a week or two to stew in my juices."

He considered that. "And after a week or two, you call me?"

She shrugged. "Yeah. It might be sooner, I don't know."

"Meanwhile, I should devote my energy to getting Kelly on the dotted line. If I get rid of wife number one, I might look more appealing to prospective wife number two."

"It wouldn't hurt," she said with a smile.

Bill took a deep breath of the misty, cold air and got onto his bike. He peered off into the distance, then looked back over his shoulder the way they'd come. "You know what? I'm going to let my true colors show. If I go back, I'm going to get to my car a hell of a lot faster than if I continue on ahead, right?"

"Yes, that's true."

He leaned over and gave her a kiss on the cheek. "You're great to look at when you're running, sweetheart, but this kid is no jock. Never was, never will be. I'll wait for you to phone." Turning the bike around, he took off, pedaling at a leisurely pace as though he hadn't a care in the world.

Christina watched him for a minute or so, then she began to run. She moved slowly at first, but gradually picked up speed. She felt free for the first time since they'd returned home. It was almost as if a burden had been lifted.

The path dropped down near the shore of the lake. Glancing at the water, she saw the eight-oared rowing shells gliding in her direction. The movement of the oarsmen was smooth, fluid, powerful. It reminded her of Robert. Lots of things the past few days had reminded her of Robert.

She hated him for exposing her weakness that last night. If they had only made love that one time she might have been able to convince herself that the passion was a fluke. But their second time had been even better than the first.

Never before had she been so eager to make love. She'd felt wild and abandoned and free. She'd wanted to give and take until there was nothing left. And even before they'd finished, she knew that somehow, in some way she didn't quite understand, she'd never be the same again.

That feeling had scared her. She'd wanted to run away, get as far from Robert Williams as she could. Bill's business crisis had been a godsend.

But even though she was home now, she was still confused and upset. The only way she knew to sort out her feelings was to buy time. Time alone. Time to reflect.

Time to find out what that indelible mark that Robert left on her was.

11

"PREGNANT?" she said. "I'm pregnant?"

Christina got up from her chair and went to the window. Dr. Joyce Koontz's private office overlooked the greenbelt behind the medical building. Beyond the parking lot, the lawn spread out for fifty yards to a new housing development. But the roofs of the homes were barely visible in the thick mist. It was raining, and had been for most of the two and a half weeks since they'd come back from Hawaii.

"I'm afraid so," Joyce replied. "We can do another test to make absolutely sure, but we just don't get false positives with the techniques we use nowadays. We get accurate readings as soon as ten days after conception."

Christina, stunned, ran the words back through her mind, testing them. She'd only been a couple of days late. Under normal circumstances that wouldn't mean a thing. But knowing she'd been with Robert, and hadn't used a diaphragm, she knew there was at least a chance that she'd gotten pregnant.

It had to have happened their second time together. At some level, she'd felt it. Without knowing exactly what it was, she'd noticed a change—that invisible mark she had felt he'd left on her. Only in a few months the mark wouldn't be so invisible. It would be a baby.

"You aren't the first woman to get pregnant on her honeymoon, Chris. I'm sure that doesn't make it any easier for you to accept, but it happens. People get carried away with the romance of it all. That's why pills aren't a bad idea."

Christina didn't reply. She just stared at her friend, diminutive, dark-headed Joyce Koontz, with her heavy-rimmed glasses and perfectly pressed lab coat.

"The news is obviously unwelcome," Joyce said when she didn't comment.

Christina felt ready to break into tears. Instead she bit her lip. "You couldn't possibly imagine."

Joyce waited, perhaps to see if she would elaborate. But Christina was still too stunned to explain. Pregnancy was not a concept she could relate to. It was something to experience in the distant future, like social security.

Even her engagement to Bill hadn't brought the notion of children to the forefront. He was not crazy about kids. She'd wanted a baby. Eventually. At the right time and place. But not now. Definitely not now.

"I can tell this has come as a big shock," Joyce said. "But I don't want you to put too much pressure on yourself over it. See a professional if you need to discuss it with someone. Bill has an obvious interest, but he doesn't have to be the only one you talk to."

Christina turned and faced the window again. Maybe Joyce was right. God knew, she didn't want to face this alone . . . and talking with someone would be a first step. Besides, Joyce was not only a friend, she was understanding and level-headed. If anyone could appreciate her dilemma, it was Joyce Koontz.

"I know this is going to come as a shock, Joyce, but—" Christina hesitated, then plunged ahead "—Bill's not the father."

Joyce gulped, but tried not to look as surprised as she undoubtedly was. "There was someone else?"

"I'm not suggesting an immaculate conception." Christina started to laugh at her own quip, but the tears that had been threatening suddenly bubbled up. She returned to her chair and picked up her purse to get some tissue. She wiped her eyes and looked at her friend. Joyce was speechless. Christina blew her nose and dabbed her eyes again.

"Do you want to talk about it?" Joyce asked.

Christina sighed. "I made love with…another man. In Hawaii. On my honeymoon with Bill."

Joyce, looking bewildered, adjusted her glasses, probably to stall for time. Finally, she glanced up at Christina. "Needless to say, I'm curious. But if you don't want to share any details, I understand."

"It was so crazy. I'm embarrassed just thinking about it." Christina took a calming breath and ran her hand back through her auburn hair. "Our first night, after the flight from hell, I got drunk, real drunk. The long and short of it is I ended up in the wrong hotel room, in the wrong bed, making love with the wrong man. I thought I was with Bill, but it was somebody else."

Joyce blinked. "You're kidding."

"Nope. It was dark. I'd had three or four Mai Tais and I was seeing double." She gave an ironic laugh. "Maybe that's why it seemed twice as good as usual."

"And the man didn't say a word?"

"He thought I was somebody else, too."

Joyce's frown moved from incredulity to skepticism.

"You'd have to have been there, believe me," Christina said. "Bottom line is, I didn't discover my mistake until morning, when I woke up and found myself in his bed. Believe me, it was a . . . let's say, unique experience."

"I can imagine."

"No. You can't."

Joyce folded her hands on the desk. "Maybe I can't," she said earnestly. "So what happened after that?"

Christina gave her the rest of the story—including the second seduction. "Robert's coming to Seattle on business soon," she said as she came to the end of her story, "and my guess is he'll want to see me. But I'm going to do my best to avoid him."

"Why?"

"Why shouldn't I? I've been embarrassed, mortified by the whole experience with him. What difference does it make that I know I'm pregnant with his child? It doesn't change my feelings about him."

"And just what are your feelings about him, Chris? Do you know?"

She shrugged. "I hardly have any. How could I? I've had three or four conversations with the guy, and it was pitch-dark half the time we were together. That barely qualifies as a fling, let alone a relationship."

"I guess you're right," Joyce said. "But if you're carrying his child, a business-as-usual attitude seems a little strange."

"You think I owe him something because he got me pregnant?"

Joyce shrugged. "Maybe not. You know best what you need to do."

Christina stopped to think about it. She pictured herself greeting Robert at the station, exchanging mild pleasantries, then taking him off to the coffee room and saying, "Oh, by the way, I'm having your child."

Actually, she didn't want to picture that little scenario.

True, she couldn't be absolutely certain how he'd react, but it was a good bet that confiding in Robert would be tantamount to giving him a piece of her. He was so hung up on fate and destiny and serendipity, so sure that he was meant to have her. And this would give him all the ammo he could possibly want. Christina could almost picture it. She'd look at him and say, "You've zapped me, big boy, now I'm yours." And he'd give her that smug, self-satisfied smile as he pulled her into his arms. She shivered at the thought. No, only silence could give her absolute control.

Christina took a deep breath. This being pregnant business had massive implications. For starters, it led to birth and a baby. An unplanned pregnancy wasn't exactly like having a root canal, losing a job or any other transient problem. When babies came, they stayed.

"There's no going back on this, is there?" she said darkly.

Joyce shook her head. "You don't have to have it, of course. And if you do, you don't have to keep it."

"Of course I'm keeping it, Joyce. I wouldn't give away my child. I'm not sixteen." Christina noticed she hadn't hesitated before replying, hadn't given the matter two thoughts. *Why?* she wondered. Was her maternal instinct that strong?

"I'm not making suggestions," Joyce said, "only presenting options."

Christina shook her head with dismay. "I can't believe I'm sitting here, having this conversation with you. Not about me. About someone else, maybe, but not me. This is something teenage girls do."

"At least you have the maturity to make a reasoned decision. And you don't have to make a decision this minute. Think about it for a while, if you want."

"I'm definitely not getting an abortion. I know that right now. Women should be able to choose, but I'm choosing not to. I can't even tell you why."

"It's good you're able to make that decision," Joyce said. "Now all you have to do is figure out how you want to manage your life, because there are changes ahead. Big changes."

Manage her life. It was a reasonable, levelheaded way of looking at it. After all, people made life-defining decisions all the time. Should I go to this college or that one? Should I choose that career or this? Which job? Where to work? Where to live? Who to live with? Who to marry?

But having a baby as an unwed mother somehow seemed different.

True, she wasn't a child having a child. She was a mature woman. But that didn't stop that panicky feeling clawing at the back of her heart. Did she really want to go through the next nine months alone?

For the first time in the two years since her mother had died, Christina had an absolutely desperate gut-wrenching desire to talk to her, to be able to put her head on Marlys Cavanaugh's shoulder and say, "Mama, what should I do?" There hadn't been many times in Christina's life when she'd felt that need—not since she was a little girl, anyway. But this was one time she really needed her mother's love, support and understanding, and couldn't have it.

There was her dad, of course, but this wasn't the sort of thing she could talk to him about. Stan Cavanaugh was a nuts-and-bolts kind of guy. He wanted to solve problems, fix things, but that wasn't what she needed right now. And, besides, she wasn't eager to tell him. That could wait until after she had all her ducks in a row.

For the moment, she had Joyce and Linda Klein—the star of her program, who was like a big sister to her—

and a couple of other women friends she could turn to. But basically, this would be a lonely undertaking. She was the one who had to have this baby. Nobody could do it for her.

Christina caught herself twisting her diamond engagement ring. What about Bill? She'd completely put him out of her mind. Pregnancy added a wrinkle to that dilemma, as well.

"Lord," she said, "I'm going to have to tell Bill, aren't I?"

"Even if you don't, he'll catch on eventually," Joyce said with a little smile.

Christina chuckled. Then she dabbed her eyes again. "Why am I laughing?"

"It helps if you can. Humor's good for the soul. That doesn't mean we're making light of it."

"Whew," Christina said with a sigh. "What a difference ten minutes can make. I'll be walking out of here a different person than the one who walked in. I hope you realize what you've done, Joyce."

"It's not what *I've* done. It's what *you* did, my sweet."

Christina stared out the window, shaking her head. "Yeah, you're right. This certainly gives new meaning to the phrase, *honeymoon from hell.* Somehow I don't think Bill is going to find our little trip so amusing anymore."

"Yes, this does put a different light on things," Joyce said.

Christina pictured Bill's face, but he didn't stay in her thoughts for long. Robert Williams was soon there. She could see him getting up from the hammock and walking toward her from the shadows of the palms. She saw his face in the moonlight. She could recall him lifting her into his arms and carrying her to his bed.

And now this. It was incredible to think that she, Christina Cavanaugh, was pregnant by him—somebody from Santa Fe, New Mexico, named Robert Williams. What did she really know about him? He was a historian and writer who'd done some work for PBS. Great. Terrific. Almost nothing.

His physical attributes were a little more familiar, of course. If she wanted to think of a man sexually, Robert came to mind much more readily than Bill. There were couples who'd been together for fifty years who hadn't had the degree of intimacy she'd known with Robert Williams in only two nights.

But everything had its price, including her Maui fling. Christina put her hand on her stomach and looked down at it, trying to fathom just what had happened to her body, what was going on in there. When she finally lifted her eyes to Joyce, they were welling with tears. She could barely see her friend's face, though Joyce could apparently read hers quite well.

"Not even the size of your fingernail," Joyce said.

Tears ran down Christina's cheeks. She dug into her purse for another tissue. By the time she'd soaked up the tears and blown her nose, it was all used up. Joyce handed her a box of tissues over the desk.

"So," Christina said, "now I go back to the office for a working lunch, giving no hint of a personal problem.

Then at home tonight, while I'm fixing dinner, I figure out how I'm going to explain this to Bill."

"You'll manage, Chris. People have more strength than they realize. You, more than most."

Christina succeeded in smiling. "Thanks for the vote of confidence."

"And if you need to talk, don't hesitate to call. At home, too, of course. Anytime, day or night."

Christina put her hand on her stomach again. "I guess you have some pamphlets and things you can give me. This womb didn't come with instructions, I'm afraid."

"We've pretty much got it down to a science these days," Joyce said. "We'll give you all the help you need, and then some. On the way out I'll give you your reading list for the course on motherhood."

Christina laughed in spite of herself—sadly, but she laughed. "If this weren't so tragic, it'd be funny."

"A baby can be a wonderful thing, even under less-than-ideal circumstances."

"Less than ideal," Christina said, repeating the phrase. "You should be writing for television, Joyce, not me."

"I'll be at your side every step of the way."

"Will you deliver the baby?"

"If you want me to."

"Of course I do."

Christina winced, biting her lip. The reality seemed to be getting harsher and more immediate by the minute.

"When do I start looking at baby clothes and lie on the floor panting?"

"Not for a while."

Christina drew a long ragged breath. "This is really happening, isn't it?"

Joyce nodded.

"Damn it," Christina said, sniffling.

"You'll be fine, Chris. You're strong."

Christina took another tissue, laughing as she blew her nose. "If a month from now you tell me I'm going to have twins, I'm going after that man with a pair of garden shears, I swear I am."

Joyce grinned. "He obviously has his attractions."

Christina put her hand on her stomach again and sighed. "Yeah. But believe me, this wasn't one."

12

"Excuse me," Robert said, rapping lightly on the open door, "are you Linda Klein?"

The woman standing at a bookcase, her back to him, turned around. She was quite tall, pretty, with shoulder-length brown hair that smoothly curved under. Robert's impression was that she was in her mid-forties, though there was something youthful about her, that suggested younger. She looked him over with the eye of a mature woman, however. "Yes, I am."

"My name's Robert Williams. I'm touring the affiliates to discuss a series I'm doing for the network and—"

"Yes, of course. I thought you looked familiar. You're the historian. The expert on the Old West."

"I did a series last year, yes."

"A wonderful program. My sons—the two still at home—loved it. Especially David, the youngest. Patrick's more into "Star Trek." In fact, several of the children in my television family talked about your program." Her eyes rounded. "Say, you wouldn't like to do a guest spot, would you? The kids would love it, I'm sure. I should talk to Christina about that. She's my producer and does quite a lot of the writing."

"Yes, I know. Actually, it's Christina I wanted to see. But she wasn't in her office, and I was told I'd probably find her here."

"Oh, forgive me, Mr. Williams. I jumped to conclusions."

"No, don't apologize. I'm intruding, I know. It's just that I was hoping to catch Christina."

"Normally you would at this time of day. We nearly always have our preshow meeting before lunch, but Christina's at the dentist's or doctor's this morning, I forget which, so we planned a working lunch." Linda Klein glanced at her watch. "She should be arriving at any moment, as a matter of fact. Did you want to wait for her, or can I help you with something?"

Robert shifted uneasily. "It's actually a personal matter, Ms. Klein. Christina wasn't expecting me today. I just got into town this morning, and was hoping to catch her... uh..."

"By surprise?"

"Yeah. To be truthful."

"What fun," Linda said, giving him a mischievous grin. "There isn't a woman alive who wouldn't enjoy being surprised by a good-looking man. Why don't you come in and have a seat."

"Thanks for the compliment. I'm not sure how Christina will feel finding me here, but I am eager to see her."

"I guess the only way to find out is to give it a try, Mr. Williams."

"Robert."

"And call me Linda." She beckoned him. "Come in and make yourself at home," she said affably. "Why not live dangerously?"

He entered the office, taking the chair she'd indicated. The place was orderly and, except for a couple of photos of the set, might as easily have been the office of a college professor.

Linda, in a white tailored silk blouse and fawn gabardine pants, sat in the guest chair opposite him. She had a sparkle and an energy that he'd expect in the hostess of a children's program. At the same time she was no Pollyanna. He could tell there was a wiliness and an intelligence underneath the chipper veneer.

"So, tell me, Robert, how do you know Christina?" she said. "Or is it impolitic of me to ask?"

"We met in Hawaii," he said, unsure whether he was venturing into dangerous waters. It was impossible to know how close Linda was to Christina or whether the story of her Hawaiian adventure had been shared with her intimates.

"Oh, on the honeymoon from hell," Linda said. "I've heard all about it."

He arched his brow. "You have?"

"Lord, yes. The flight, the baggage, the room, the busboy, the rental car. It was the talk of the station for a few days." She glanced toward the door. "But don't tell Christina I said so. The poor thing doesn't know how much fun we had with it."

Robert had his answer. Either Linda was oblivious, or she was being very discreet.

"You met Bill, then," Linda said.

"Yes."

"Sweet guy, isn't he?"

"Yes."

Robert wasn't up for small talk. In fact, he didn't want to talk at all. For the past few days all he could think about was Christina. He badly needed to find out what her current state of mind was. And it was not at all reassuring to hear her colleague speaking so positively about Bill Roberts.

"So, how are Christina and Bill doing?" he asked innocently. "I know they were upset to have to cut their trip short."

Linda shrugged. "I assume they're fine. Christina hasn't talked about Bill much. He's wrapped up in some big negotiation in California. I believe he's been down there for over a week."

Robert brightened at the news. "Oh, really?"

"So, will you be in Seattle long?" she asked.

"I don't know. This is the last town on my tour. I was planning on taking some time off. I just haven't decided who with and where."

"We'd love to have a man of your stature contribute to the show," she said. "Christina has put the main focus for this year on retelling ancient myths. The kids really love it and they get to learn a little something while they're being entertained, too. If you were willing to get involved, we could do some fascinating things with the whole Native American culture."

"Yes, that could be interesting," he said, aware of the open door and the possibility that Christina could appear any moment. Distracted, he let the conversation lapse into silence.

"I suppose you and Christina had fun talking shop," Linda said, making conversation, "you both being in the business and all."

"Actually we didn't talk much about TV."

"Really? She's so passionate about the show, I'd have thought she'd have bent your ear. She not only produces it, she does most of the writing, you know. I'd have thought the two of you would have compared a lot of notes."

"Actually, she hadn't seen my series."

"I'm surprised. It was the talk of the station for several months. Christina isn't big on station politics, though. She'd much rather write a script. She only got into the production end at my insistence. She's a clear thinker, organized, bright. If one of my two older boys came home from college with a girl like her, I'd be delighted, positively delighted."

"Believe me, I know what you mean," Robert said, perhaps more wistfully than was wise.

"She's lovely, isn't she?"

"Beautiful."

"She could have done anything in the world of modeling that she wanted," Linda said, "but her creative drive was just too strong. Beauty, talent, brains. Christina's quite a package!"

Oddly, Robert hadn't seen the creative side of Christina. Yet, in a way, he wasn't surprised. From the first moment he'd seen her, he was sure she was perfect for him. This was simply more proof that they were meant for each other.

"And she's wonderfully in sync with the minds of kids," Linda went on. "Writing for children is actually very difficult."

"It's funny," he said, glancing toward the door, "but Christina and children don't readily go together in my mind. Maybe it's because I don't know her that well."

"Her talents are diverse. I've seen some of the poetry she has written just for fun. It's quite good. Her scripts for the show are lively, funny, imaginative. In a word, terrific! And that's not just a children's show host speaking. I taught college literature before I got into TV."

"Really?"

Linda checked her watch again. "Where is that girl? I hope she didn't end up having a tooth pulled." She drummed her nails on the armchair. "Listen, Robert, I've got to pick up revisions for today's script before my meeting with Christina. Would you mind if I left you for a few minutes?"

"No, but I don't have to wait. I can catch Christina later, after your meeting."

"Don't be silly. She'll want to see you. In fact, why don't you have lunch with us? Christina and I can go over our business while you have your salad, and then maybe the three of us can talk about your doing a guest appearance on the show. Knowing Chris, she'll have some ideas."

He took a deep breath and slowly exhaled. "I'm sure she will."

Linda got up. "I'll only be a few minutes. If Christina comes, tell her I'll be right back." She put her hand on his shoulder as she passed by and quickly left the room.

He listened as the sound of her heels faded up the hall. Robert sat there, feeling rather pleased with himself. It was damned reassuring to know that Bill was out of town. That gave him an extra advantage. Not that he'd doubted that fate was on his side, but Christina was being stubborn about seeing it. He was in for a struggle to prove it to her. No doubt about it.

As he waited, Robert again heard the sound of heels in the hall. Was it Linda coming back already, or was it Christina?

CHRISTINA SAW Linda's open door and slowed down. She'd run up the stairs because the elevators were tied up, but she didn't want to enter the office panting. She pictured Linda sitting on the corner of her desk, purse slung over her shoulder, coat over her arm, that elfin grin, and saying something like, "Oh, good, I was afraid they'd gotten you mixed up with a heart-transplant patient." They'd both laugh and then hurry off to lunch.

Christina had halfway decided to tell Linda about her pregnancy sooner rather than later. The quicker she got it off her chest, the better. Then she wouldn't have to agonize. And Linda, with her various children and life experience, would be understanding.

"Sorry," Christina said, coming through the doorway, "I—" The sight of him sitting there brought her up short. Her mouth sagged open. "Oh."

Robert got to his feet. "Hello, Christina."

His eyes moved down her body. His tongue darted out to moisten his full lower lip. Christina knew he wasn't just admiring the way her rust cashmere dress clung to her. He was remembering every moment of the way it had been between them. She was momentarily speechless.

"Linda went to pick up the revised script," he said. "She'll be right back."

"What are you doing here?" They were the only words that came to mind.

"Interviewing for a guest slot on the show," he said with a smile.

"What?"

"It was Linda's idea, not mine."

"How do you know Linda?"

"I don't. That is, I just met her. Nice lady. Very nice lady."

Christina was too stunned to make sense of anything. She could only stare at him. Robert looked somehow different in a sport coat and tie. Respectable. It was a shock seeing him, especially after the news she'd just gotten. She wasn't at all sure she was up to this.

"You just walked in and introduced yourself?"

"Actually, I was told I'd find you here. I wanted to say hello."

Christina had the strangest desire to turn and run, to go as fast and as far from there as she could. But she felt an equally strong impulse to stay. Robert Williams lured her and threatened her at the same time, a moth-to-a-flame sort of thing. In the end, inertia kept her where she was.

"You don't seem terribly pleased to see me," he said.

"I . . . I didn't think I'd see you again."

"Well, we didn't get to say goodbye when you left Maui. Not properly, anyway."

He moved toward her, the look in his eye every bit as purposeful as the night he'd gotten her pregnant. Christina felt herself tense. Again, she had a strong impulse to turn and run. But she held her ground.

"You look terrific, by the way," he said.

"Thanks."

"It's the first time we've seen each other dressed like grown-ups," he said.

"Yes, most of the time we were together, I didn't have a stitch on," she replied. She nervously shifted her trench coat to her other arm.

"It's nice to see you can joke about it."

"I don't know why I did. God knows, it's not funny." She unconsciously started to lay the flat of her hand against her stomach, then caught herself. "More like tragic."

"I see you're still wearing Bill's ring." There was an edge to his voice.

Christina glanced down at the diamond. "Yes."

"You decided not to tell him, apparently."

She took a deep breath, weighing the possibility of admitting all was not well in engagement land. But there was no doubt in her mind that it would encourage him, and that was the last thing she wanted. She was still considering how best to answer when Robert spoke again.

"I take it your silence means that Bill's still in the dark and that I'm not exactly welcome here." He paused to look deeply into her eyes. "I thought maybe our second night together would change things. Make you realize you had to tell him."

The mere mention of that night made Christina so weak that she had to sit. Without answering, she hung her coat on Linda's rack, then sat in the chair Robert had been in. What was it about this man that made him able to zero in on her greatest weakness? And it *did* have to be him. Surely being pregnant wasn't taking its toll this quickly.

Robert must have taken her sitting as an invitation to talk, because he pulled another chair close to hers and sat down. She rubbed her forehead, wondering how she could possibly deal with him now—less than a half hour after finding out that she was pregnant. By him.

"What do you expect from me, Robert? Am I supposed to throw my arms around you and give you a big kiss?"

"That would be nice."

She looked up at him, so frustrated that she felt like bursting into tears.

"All right," he said, "I can see by your reaction you consider me a horrible person. But do me a favor... tell me my sin. I'd like the pleasure of knowing why I'm going down in flames. Was it because I happened to be the guy in that room you walked into? Was it because I created problems for you with Bill? Or was it because I was less than a gentleman and took advantage of you that last evening?"

"I'd say all of that pretty well sums it up. As I told you that first morning, I wanted you to disappear so that I wouldn't have to deal with you. That hasn't changed." Lord, she thought, was that ever true. Especially now.

He stroked his chin. "Does that mean you won't have dinner with me this evening?"

Christina rolled her eyes. "You don't get it, do you?"

"I get it. I'm just not crazy about the script."

"Sorry about that," she said, trying to sound firm, "but what is, is."

"I hear the words, but I just don't believe you. I don't think you dislike me as much as you let on. I think the real problem is that you're afraid to trust your own feelings."

He sounded so convincing that she was almost ready to give in. Almost. She studied him, feeling annoyed, angry, upset and confused all at the same time. Why he made her emotions bounce around like a Ping-Pong ball, she didn't know.

She'd dreaded seeing him again, especially considering the news Joyce had given her. A part of her wasn't even sure that she would tell him about the baby. And the worst of it was that no matter how hard she tried to be calm and logical, her emotions were always in high gear whenever they were together. She was either making love with the man, or bickering with him, or on the verge of tears.

"I'm sorry," she said softly. "You picked an unfortunate time to show up. This has been a bad day for me. A terrible day, as a matter of fact."

The words were no sooner out than her eyes flooded. Embarrassed for having allowed herself to get emotional in front of him, Christina grabbed a tissue from her purse and dabbed her eyes. She glanced at Robert. He looked distressed.

"I didn't mean to upset you," he said, the concern in his voice evident.

"It has nothing to do with you," she replied, before realizing how absurd that was. "I mean, nothing you said."

"Well, if it wasn't anything I said, was it something I did? Besides making love with you, I mean."

Again, he'd zeroed in on the crux of the problem. Robert unpeeled her defenses like a chef going through the layers of an artichoke on his way to the heart. He was relentless. How could she stand up to that kind of scrutiny? Especially now? She had half a mind to tell him she was pregnant. If nothing else, it might put things into perspective.

But of course she couldn't. She hadn't even come to terms with the problem herself. To Joyce, she had talked like she was ready to start laying in a supply of diapers, but Christina knew she hadn't thought the situation through. Not really. In a way, she'd embraced the notion of having a baby as readily as Robert had embraced the notion of having a relationship. And neither of them knew what they were doing.

She sniffled, blowing her nose. Embarrassed by her emotion, she apologized. "Sorry. I'm not usually like this. You'll have to forgive me."

"Creative people are emotional by definition. If you can't feel, you can't convey feelings to others."

"By that standard, I should be a romance writer."

"Linda said you write wonderful poetry."

"Linda is generous with her praise. She's my big sister and surrogate mother all rolled into one. And I'm the kid sister she never had."

"Sounds like a nice relationship."

"I love working with her. And I like writing for the show. Kids can be—" her voice faded "—a lot of fun."

"You like children then."

Christina felt the color drain from her face. Her mouth went dry. Strange that such an otherwise innocuous comment should affect her so strongly.

"I . . . always thought I'd have some, I guess," she murmured.

"Yeah, me, too."

Her stomach tightened. This conversation was getting much too close to home. Had she the strength, she might have gotten up and walked from the room.

"I almost did once," he said. "My wife died because of an ectopic pregnancy. It makes the whole issue a rather emotional one for me."

Christina winced, involuntarily clasping her arms to her stomach. Tears came again, glossing her eyes, then running down her face. But she didn't bother to wipe them away. The pain she felt was for him as much as for herself. "I didn't know you'd been married."

"Laura's been gone for a long time now. It'll be five years soon."

"Oh, Robert," she whispered, "I had no idea. I'm so sorry."

Seeing her tears, he handed her his handkerchief. "I didn't tell you in a bid for sympathy," he said.

Christina wiped her cheeks and returned the handkerchief. She drew an uneven breath. "You could say almost anything and I'd cry. Like I told you, it's been a rough day." She glanced at the door. "I wonder where Linda is? We're supposed to go to lunch. I'm sure she told you we've got to meet about today's show."

Robert cleared his throat. "Yes, as a matter of fact, she thought maybe . . . we could . . ."

They heard the clatter of heels in the hall and Linda came running in with a handful of papers. Robert got to his feet. So did Christina.

"Oh, thank goodness you're here, Chris," she said, hurrying to her desk. "Word processing screwed up and amended the changes to yesterday's script. What a mess." She stuffed papers into a folio lying on the desk. "But everything's copacetic now." She looked at the two of them. "Well, shall we go? If we hurry we can have a good meal and I can still get back in time."

Christina and Robert looked at each other.

"Didn't Robert tell you about the wonderful idea I had about having him as a guest on the show?" she said to Christina. "We were going to discuss it over lunch. I invited him to join us."

"I mentioned it in passing," Robert said, glancing at Christina.

"Well, let's get going," Linda said.

"You know, Linda, I think I'll pass," Robert said. "You're pressed for time. Maybe Christina will let me take her to lunch tomorrow and we can discuss it then."

The women looked at each other. Christina didn't know whether to reject the suggestion outright or accede to his wishes.

"I'll have to check my calendar," she said, stalling. "Call me later."

Linda got her coat from the rack and headed for the door. "Handle it as you like," she said, "but let's figure out a way to do it. The kids will love Robert. I have a hunch. Sorry to run like this," she said to him. "See yourself out, if you don't mind. Come on, Chris."

Christina had gotten her coat and followed her, glancing back at Robert before she went out the door. He was smiling slightly, but not gloating. That, at least, was an improvement.

It took her a few steps to catch up with Linda. "I have one question," she said. "Was his being on the show really your idea or was it his?"

"It was mine. Why?"

"I just wondered if he'd engineered it. I wouldn't have put it past him."

Linda gave her a strange look. "Is something going on between you two that I'm missing?"

Christina gulped, realizing she'd been too direct. "No, Robert's just . . . rather . . . assertive."

They came to the elevator. A car arrived almost at once. They stepped in. Christina leaned against the side of the car, feeling weak. Linda studied her.

"Assertive, maybe, but a damn fine specimen," she said.

"Yes, I guess he is."

"Must be a real heartbreaker."

Christina looked at her with surprise. "Why do you say that?"

"He either had you crying, or the dentist did."

Christina touched her cheeks, realizing she probably looked like hell. "I wasn't at the dentist. It was the
gynecologist."

The elevator stopped on the ground floor and they
stepped out, heading for the entrance.

"No bad news, I hope," Linda said under her breath.

Christina didn't answer. They both put on their coats
and went outside into the mist. Linda glanced at her as
they went up the sidewalk.

"You aren't going to tell me you're pregnant, are
you?" Linda said out of the blue.

"I haven't decided if I'll tell you or not."

Linda did a double take. "You're kidding."

Christina said nothing.

"Are you pregnant?"

Christina glanced at her but couldn't speak.

"Oh, my," Linda said.

"You got that right," Christina said weakly.

Linda took her arm. "Whatever's happened, you
have my support, one hundred percent."

Christina bit her lip, feeling the tears threaten once
again. "Thanks."

They walked for a while in silence. Christina could
tell that Linda was dying to know what had happened.
She struggled to find a way to begin. She finally blurted
out, "It's his."

"Robert's?"

Christina nodded.

"Oh, my God. Bill has no idea, I imagine?"

Christina shook her head.

Linda gave her arm a squeeze. "You're going to need all the support you can get."

Christina sniffled, stifling a sob. Linda dug a handkerchief out of her pocket and handed it to her.

"The first is the hardest," she said. "They come easier after that. As the mother of four sons, I know, believe me."

13

CHRISTINA WENT JOGGING in a driving rain before work the next morning. Usually, on weekdays, she ran after work to get rid of stress before dinner, but when she woke up an hour earlier than usual, she decided to put in some miles. Joyce had told her to continue her normal routine, except to cut out alcohol. That wasn't going to be a sacrifice. She hadn't had a drop since Maui.

As she ran, Christina monitored her body. She'd thought about her physical condition a lot. Before going to bed she'd stood naked in front of a full-length mirror, trying to envision herself eight or nine months pregnant. She could do it, but it seemed as unreal as sprouting wings and beginning to fly. More than once she wondered if it was all a joke, some kind of terrible mistake.

The previous evening had been her first real chance to think seriously about the baby—and put Robert's visit in perspective—since work had kept her fairly busy. All day she had looked forward to having some alone time. But when she'd finally found herself in the relative quiet of her condo, she'd felt lonely and scared. Thank God, her friends had come to her rescue.

Joyce had called and they'd talked for half an hour, mostly about working while pregnant, though they'd also discussed child care and the options Christina would have.

Then Linda had phoned. At lunch they'd had to take care of business, given the time pressure before the show, so they had a lot to say to each other when she called, too.

Reaching the top of a hillock, Christina stopped to take a rest. Normally she didn't do that, but she was feeling weaker than usual. Joyce had said she'd experience a loss of energy.

Christina took a few deep breaths, keeping her back to the driving rain, then started slowly down the hill. She seldom ran with anyone, but this morning she'd have liked someone to spur her on.

She thought again of her conversation with Linda. She was glad she'd told her about Robert since that gave her someone to talk to who'd actually met him. To Joyce, he'd been an abstraction. Linda, at least, knew the flesh-and-blood person.

"I like him," Linda had said.

"Do you?"

"Yes. There's something very real and down-to-earth about him, something...I don't know...solid and wholesome."

"Robert is no Boy Scout, Linda, believe me."

"I didn't say he wasn't sexy. In fact, he's very appealing. But there are certain men who are both charismatic and decent—you know, good guys. Believe me,

Chris, having two ex-husbands, four sons, and dealing with all their friends, teams, clubs, et cetera, et cetera, I know about men. The special ones you can pick out immediately. I'd say Robert is one."

"I have to admit my impression of him was different today than in Hawaii."

"How so?"

"It probably wasn't fair, but in Maui I saw him as a predator. Since coming home, I've come to the realization I wasn't as upset with him as I was with myself for having fallen prey so easily."

"And now?"

"He told me his wife died of a tubal pregnancy. Hearing that, my whole attitude changed. That isn't rational, I know. He's the same man as before, but somehow I saw him differently."

"Empathy."

"Maybe. But I've decided I have to keep a clear head. I can't get emotional. I'm still the woman I was before I got pregnant."

"So, what does that mean?"

"I don't know," she'd said. "I'm still trying to figure things out."

Linda had laughed. Christina had, too, even though it was a bit like whistling in the dark. Whenever she stopped to remind herself that her life had in fact changed, she was a little scared.

Running along the edge of the lake, the rain pounding on her back, she couldn't help seeing the future as daunting. She felt isolated and alone—one woman against the elements, one woman against life. Or so it seemed.

She finally made it back to her condo, soaked and generally feeling miserable. Her body heat from the exercise kept her from getting chilled, but the hot shower felt wonderful. She stood under the pounding spray, evaluating herself and her feelings.

She was a woman with child. How long, she wondered, would it be before she fully accepted that reality without constantly having to remind herself that it was true? Would it take until her stomach got big?

While she had her coffee she walked around her one-bedroom place, mug in hand, trying to find comfort in the familiarity of her things. The condo was small, pleasantly decorated and comfortable. Her dad had let her have her choice of her mother's things and she'd taken a writing desk, which she kept in the front room, a sideboard, which was really too big for the tiny dining area, and an antique chest, which was in the bedroom. Otherwise her furniture and decor was modest — some of it, like her oil paintings, the product of her regular expeditions to the flea markets around town.

Her king bed was top quality, if too large for the room, a present from Bill, who'd hated her old double bed both for being too small and too soft. He valued his sleep and had strong preferences where he did it. There was a finicky side to Bill Roberts.

She had a picture of him on her bookcase. She went over to look at it. There was no question that the pregnancy would be a death knell for their relationship.

During the sleepless hours of night she wondered if maybe her decision to have the baby might not have been made at least partly with that in mind. Maybe deep down she didn't want to marry Bill and never truly had. What better way to kiss a man off than get pregnant by somebody else?

The ironic thing was that by ending things with Bill, she was left high and dry. She had been self-sufficient before she'd met Bill; she was self-sufficient during their relationship; and now that they were parting company, she would be more needy and vulnerable than at any time in her life. Funny, the way life worked.

The telephone rang, breaking her reverie. Christina went to the kitchen to answer. Ironically, it was Bill calling from San Francisco.

"Hope I'm not phoning too early," he said, "but I wanted to catch you before you went to the office."

"No problem. I've been up for hours. I've already been for a run."

"I leave town for a week and you become a morning person?"

"I was up, so I figured, why not?"

"I've got to tell you, Chris, I really miss you."

Christina played the words over in her head. Normally they would have made her feel good. Now they struck her as sad. Poor Bill seemed pathetic to her, though he'd done nothing to warrant it.

"But there's good news," he went on. "I'm going to be able to get out of here a few days earlier than I thought. I'll be back in Seattle tomorrow afternoon.

And since we haven't seen each other for a while, I thought maybe you'd let me take you to dinner."

Christina had an impulse to tell him what had happened, but she knew she couldn't do that to him. Not over the phone. It wasn't fair. She owed him the decency of a face-to-face conversation.

"Actually that might be a good idea," she said. "I want to talk to you and tomorrow over dinner would be good."

He hesitated. "Should I read something ominous in your tone?"

"More like a desire to be candid and respectful, Bill."

"I don't know if that's any better."

She anguished. "Let me put it this way—we haven't talked for a while and I think we should. But you don't have to take me out. I can fix some spaghetti or something."

"Okay. I'll supply the wine," he said. "How's that?"

"Whatever you like, Bill."

"What time?"

"Seven?"

"Sold. See you tomorrow night."

Christina hung up with a heavy heart. She felt as if her life was hurtling down a strange new path, and she was without the power to change its course. Ever since they'd agreed to go on that damned honeymoon from hell, her future had seemed to be in the grip of a powerful, ineluctable force. Nothing was the same. Fate had turned the world upside down.

AT NOON Christina stood just inside the entrance of the building where the station was located, waiting for Robert. He'd called her office first thing that morning to set their luncheon appointment. He and the station manager would be returning from a meeting downtown with a public relations firm, so they'd agreed the lobby would be a convenient place to meet.

Christina had agonized all morning. She had two awful tasks to get through that day—telling Bill she'd gotten pregnant on their honeymoon, and deciding what to do about Robert. He seemed determined that they get to know each other, and she'd been equally determined never to see him again. But that was before yesterday. What did she do today?

Her other concern about Robert was deciding what obligation—moral or otherwise—she had to tell him about the baby. Her initial plan had been to stick with her first impulse and keep him in the dark. At least that way, once he left town and was out of her life, she wouldn't have to think about him.

But during her long sleepless night, she'd given some thought to their child, wondering if it didn't have something at stake in the decision. When the baby got older and began asking questions about its father, did she name names? If so, the only decent thing to do would be to let Robert know first, prepare him. But did that mean she should tell him now or later?

Christina hadn't the vaguest idea how to go about telling a virtual stranger that he'd gotten her pregnant. And she had even less idea how a man could be expected to react to news of that ilk. The implications were not without consequence. There were financial considerations, if nothing else. Not that she expected Robert to support the child—she'd prefer it if he didn't.

Christina was so lost in thought that she wasn't immediately aware that someone had come up beside her. Turning, she saw that it was Robert. She blinked, almost as though she hadn't expected him.

He had a smile on his face, one indicating delight. She stared at him for a second or two, taking him in, processing what she was seeing before finally managing to gather her wits.

"Oh. I didn't see you come up."

"You were obviously off somewhere," he said, "and I didn't want to break the spell."

Christina was embarrassed. "I guess I was preoccupied."

"Has anyone ever told you you're lovely when you're preoccupied?"

"Compliments right out of the chute?"

"Sure, why not? They're sincere."

He had an easy affability that had escaped her in the past. Maybe she'd always been so much on the defensive that she hadn't appreciated that. And he did look good. She had noticed that every time she'd seen him—though she'd always been quick to discount it. Maybe she'd picked up some of Linda's objectivity. Maybe it made a difference to think of him as a good guy for a change.

Robert's hair was damp from the mist. And the cold air had colored his cheeks. He also had a happy twinkle in his eye. His smile made her feel good.

"Shall we go?" he said.

Christina nodded and he took her arm. She went off with him, not exactly feeling carefree, but with a lighter heart than before. It seemed crazy, but then, this man had already proven that he could do strange things to her mind.

Robert suggested they go to the waterfront, because he felt like "looking at some sea gulls." Christina volunteered to drive even though he was prepared to take a taxi. As they pulled onto the street from the parking garage, she asked him why the sudden allure of sea gulls.

"I don't know," he said, "maybe I like to watch them soar. Maybe it's the way I feel today."

Christina couldn't imagine why he felt like soaring, but she remembered that was the way he'd made her feel the night of their first encounter. She'd thought of that a lot recently, and of the next night, too, though mostly with doubt and regret. Those same memories today, if not bringing greater pleasure, at least brought far less remorse.

Christina glanced over at him when she came to a stoplight. He was watching her with that self-assured smile of his—the one that told her he was absolutely sure they were meant for each other. He reached over and took the ends of her hair between his fingers.

"Do you realize this is our first date?" he said.

"Date?"

"For want of a better term. You know what I mean, seeing each other under ordinary circumstances, having a conversation in pleasant surroundings."

"We're going out to lunch to discuss Linda's idea of having you on the show, not to socialize."

"That may be why *you're* here. I have better things to talk about."

"Too bad, because I want to talk about the show."

"Then we'll get that out of the way first, so you won't have to feel guilty. I think I'd be a lousy guest. I'm no actor. In front of the camera I tend to be stiff and...I don't know...cerebral. Henry Kissinger would do better."

"Put yourself in pretty rarefied company, don't you, Robert?"

He laughed. "Well, you know the male ego, Christina. No false modesty here." He gave her a wink. "But to get back to my point, Linda's way off base if she thinks I'd do well with a bunch of kids, whether the subject is cowboys and Indians or not."

"You'd know better than I," she said.

"I don't want to hurt her feelings, because I know she meant it as a compliment, but neither do I want to embarrass everybody—her especially."

"You might be underestimating yourself. Linda has good instincts. You'd be surprised who's been on the show and done well."

"Has she had Kissinger on yet?"

"No. We thought we'd start a little lower on the food chain."

"Touché," Robert said, giving her a tap on the shoulder.

Christina laughed and he did, too. She brought the car to a stop at another light. They looked into each other's eyes, still laughing. She could feel a strong impulse of attraction running between them. Memories of Hawaii streamed through her mind. That unnerved her. She broke eye contact, peering ahead at the light.

"Ever been to Santa Fe?" he asked.

They were moving again. "No."

"Well, you'll love it."

"Whoa," she said, giving him a sideways glance. "Aren't we skipping along a little fast? We were just weighing your appeal to kids as compared to Henry Kissinger's and suddenly you have me going to your hometown."

"Why not? Sounds perfectly reasonable to me."

"Knowing you, it would."

"I'll ignore the sarcasm and tell you how much I want you to see my ranch, instead."

"You have a ranch? You mean you're a *real* cowboy?"

"It's a small spread, near town. Just under a thousand acres."

"Incredible," she said. "I've slept with you twice and only now do I find out you're a buckaroo."

"That might be overstating the case, Christina. I fall somewhere between a city slicker and the real McCoy.

Some of my neighbors call me 'the professor,' but they still invite me to their barbecues."

"Do you have a horse?"

"Three."

"I guess that means hat and boots, as well."

"One and two, respectively. But I don't wear either of them in Hawaii, or on the road when I'm pitching my programs, for that matter."

She chuckled. "Boy, you think you know someone and then you discover you don't know them at all," she said. "Any other deep, dark, shocking secrets I should know about?"

"No, actually not. What you see is pretty much what you get."

"What about your personal life?" she asked. "There's no one special?"

"If you mean a special lady, the answer is no. I've seen a few women over the years since Laura died. I have friends, but no one I care about. Until I met you, that is."

Christina had no reason to be surprised by the remark, given his consistency on the point, but his certainty about her always brought her up short. How could he be so sure about his feelings when they were only just now getting acquainted?

"I've half expected there never would be another special woman," he went on.

"Really?"

"You sound surprised."

"Robert, I'll be honest. You strike me as someone who's been around."

"Hmm. Let me make sure I understand. Are you trying to insult me, or give me a compliment?"

"I don't know. Both, I guess."

He laughed. "You can't decide what you think of me, can you?"

"Does everybody have this trouble?" she asked. "Or is it only me?"

"You're the first who's ever complained, let me put it that way."

They'd come to the Alaskan Way, which ran along the waterfront. Christina spotted a parking spot and grabbed it. She turned off the engine. Glancing over at him, she sighed. "Well, here we are."

Robert was giving her that same smug look again—the one that told her they belonged together, whether she realized it or not. He reached over and brushed her cheek with the back of his finger, the way he had that second night they were together in the moonlight, outside his bungalow at the Coral Reef. In spite of herself, Christina felt herself weaken just at the way he looked at her.

"You keep surprising me," she said, taking his hand and holding it.

"Do I?"

She nodded.

"Maybe it's your turn to surprise me," he said. "Anything you want to tell me about yourself that'll knock me on my heels?"

She was silent for a long time, looking out at the patches of blue sky between the broken clouds. She knew he was watching her intently, but she also knew he couldn't possibly imagine what was going through her mind.

Finally she said, "Well, I'm pregnant. Does that qualify?"

14

FOR A SECOND Robert wasn't sure he'd heard right. She'd said "pregnant," hadn't she?

"Did you say you were pregnant?"

"Yes."

"I thought that's what you said."

He tried to sort out the implications. Christina was having a baby. But whose baby? That was the question. A slow smile spread across his face as he realized it had to be his. Otherwise she wouldn't have told him...at least not like that. She'd have said, "Forget me, because *Bill* and I are having a baby."

He turned to her, a big grin spreading across his face. "It's mine, isn't it? You got pregnant in Hawaii?"

"What makes you think so?"

Her voice was even, though a touch defensive. But the most telling part was that she wouldn't meet his gaze. He *was* right. She was having *his* baby! "Because it just *has* to be. Don't you see, Christina, this was meant to be. Just like you getting in my bed—"

"The *wrong* bed," she said flatly.

He shook his head. "No. The *right* bed. It was the right woman in the right bed with the right man."

When she didn't say anything, he felt a sudden crisis of confidence. "Or are you going to tell me that I'm wrong...and it's Bill's?"

Christina shook her head and gazed up the street at the traffic. "No. That's not too likely. We didn't even make love in Hawaii, and before that we always used something. We were very careful. Both of us. So unless you've had a vasectomy or you're sterile..."

"No on both counts."

She looked over at him, blinking away a tear. Then she swallowed hard. "It's yours, then."

Robert felt a wave of relief wash over him. For a moment he'd felt real fear—fear that the baby might be Bill's, fear that his dream might be slipping away. Fate wasn't always kind. After all, he'd lost Laura...and their child.

But now providence had given him a second chance at love, and a family. It was a gift from the gods. "This is wonderful," he said, a smile creeping across his face.

"You're pleased?" she said, sounding astonished.

"Of course I'm pleased."

"How can you be! Robert, this kind of thing isn't supposed to happen to mature, responsible adults. I did a terrible, stupid thing letting you make love to me."

"No," he said, taking her hand. "Please don't say that. Don't you see, it makes perfect sense. Our meeting, making love, making a baby...it's like a fairy tale."

"Oh, God. I can't believe this. Don't you see we're talking tragedy here?"

"We're obviously not looking at this the same way," he said, growing concerned.

"Now there's something we can agree on."

The words were angry, defensive. But Robert was almost sure she wasn't mad. She was scared. She had begun to tear up again. He squeezed her fingers as a tear slid over her lid and down her cheek. He leaned over and kissed her, tasting the salt. Christina gave him a woeful look and reached down to the floor of the car for her purse. She took a tissue and wiped her eyes.

"I haven't cried so much in all my life," she said. "At the drop of a hat, it seems. I guess it's part of being pregnant."

"When did you find out?"

"Yesterday. Half an hour before I saw you."

"Lord," he said with a sigh. "Then you're just getting used to the idea and I show up."

She nodded.

"Does Bill know?"

"No. He's in California. I couldn't tell him over the phone. He'll be back tomorrow. I'll tell him then."

"How's he going to react?"

"How would you react?" she replied.

He chuckled. "How am I reacting?"

"Right, dumb question," she said. "You're obviously pleased as punch. Must be a male thing. You zapped me and you can feel good about yourself."

He kissed her fingers, one at a time. "I am pleased, but I'm not as cavalier as you might think. I'm sorry if I gave you that impression."

He took another deep breath as he gathered his thoughts. "I've been through this once before, you know—thought I was going to have a child. But it didn't happen." He put his arm around her shoulder and gave it a squeeze. "This time will be different. You'll be fine. I promise I won't let anything happen to you."

"Now just a minute, Robert. Let's not get ahead of ourselves. I might be pregnant but you are not my husband."

"Maybe not, but a father has rights . . . and responsibilities. I'm certainly not going to shirk mine. I want to be clear about that right up front."

Christina pulled away from him, gripping the steering wheel. "Oh, no. This is my problem. It has nothing to do with you."

"It has a great deal to do with me. This baby is mine, too, isn't it?"

She gave him a distressed look. "Robert, you aren't going to give me a bad time about this, are you?"

"Bad time? No. I'm going to meet my responsibilities, though."

Her face fell. She clearly seemed upset by his response.

"That doesn't please you, does it?"

"I'd never have told you if I'd known you were going to be difficult," she replied.

He touched her arm. "Christina, I'm trying to be supportive."

She sniffled. He took her tissue from her and dabbed her cheek. Then he kissed her lightly. Looking into her glistening eyes, he felt such a well of love. A lump formed in his throat. He felt protective of her. He couldn't help himself. His eyes began to shimmer.

"When I saw you at the Coral Reef that first evening with the wind blowing your hair, you seemed like a goddess," he said. "I couldn't possibly have imagined that I'd be here with you now and we'd be talking about having a child. It has to be destiny. Nothing else could possibly explain it."

"You're such a dreamer, Robert. You're idealizing the situation, just as you've idealized me."

"Maybe. But you've never looked more beautiful to me than you do right now."

She searched his eyes. "That is a sweet thing to say," she murmured. "Even for a hopeless romantic."

Then, much to his surprise, she leaned over and kissed him on the lips, taking his face in her hands, much as he had hers.

"But there is one problem," she added.

"What's that?"

"My doctor told me I had to eat properly. Balanced diet, no skipping meals and so forth."

"You're saying you're hungry."

"Robert, I could eat a horse."

"Make that a steer," he said. "We buckaroos think of our horses as our friends."

She laughed, looking happy for the first time. "You really ride and rope and brand cows and do all that stuff?"

"I do a lot of supervising, let's put it that way." A thought came to him as he gazed through the windshield at the patchy sky. "You know what, I'm going to have to buy a pony now, aren't I?"

She rolled her eyes. "That does it," she said, opening the car door. "I'm going to lunch. I'm going to buy myself a nice big *salmon* steak. If you want to sit here and romanticize this thing, you'll have to do it alone."

"Hold on," he said, opening his door. "I can do salmon, too."

As he came around the car, Christina gave him an admonishing look. He put his arm around her shoulders and they crossed the street, headed for the Pike Place Market. He gestured toward the sky.

"Looks like we're finally getting a break in the weather. Maybe it's an omen."

LINDA KLEIN closed the script binder, looking across her desk at Christina. "Well, that pretty much finishes the tale about how King Arthur found Excalibur. I guess we should either move on to Greek myths or try for a bit of the Southwest. What did Robert say about doing a guest spot with some Native American stories?"

"He doesn't think he'd be good."

"Don't tell me he hates children."

"Actually, he's thrilled with the idea of having one."

Linda's eyes rounded. "You told him?"

"It just slipped out."

"You two are a rather accident-prone pair, aren't you?"

Christina smiled. "Seems that way, doesn't it?"

Linda pointed at Christina's hands folded in her lap. "Any significance to the fact that Bill's ring is no longer on your finger?"

"At lunch Robert asked me to take it off."

"My, Robert's stock seems to be rising rapidly."

"Well, he was right. It's hypocritical to wear Bill's ring. Even he would be embarrassed."

"You seem pretty sure of that."

"Linda, I'm not sure of anything. I'm running on instinct. I don't know what it is about Robert, but whichever way I turn, whatever I do, he's there—whether by accident or design. It happened in Hawaii, it's happening here. It's like I'm on this gigantic, sticky spiderweb and there he sits, right in the middle of it."

Linda suppressed a smile. "So that's the origin of that little fly-and-spider story in today's tell-and-draw segment." She checked her watch. "Well, I've got to run. Patrick and David have been promised dinner out tonight. Moms must always keep their word."

"I used to let these bon mots of yours pass without giving them two thoughts," Christina said. "Now I'm thinking I should start taking notes."

They both laughed. "Most parenting is done by the seat of the pants. It doesn't hurt to get a tip or two along the way, though. Either that, or have several kids. The first few don't need to know you're practicing on them."

"Thanks," Christina said, "but I'd rather not look beyond number one."

They both got up and put on their coats.

"I've got errands to do on the way home," Christina said, "so I'm glad you want to leave early. I'm picking up two big juicy steaks at the grocery store."

Linda gave her a double take. "Joyce may have told you that you were eating for two, kiddo, but I don't think that's what she had in mind."

Christina gave her a chiding look. "I'm having a guest for dinner."

"Oh? Anyone I know?"

"Know any cowboy historians?"

"We seem to be moving right along, don't we? Next thing I know you'll be humming 'Home on the Range.'"

"No, it's nothing like that. It's just that Robert and I are in the same boat," Christina said as they went out the door. "He suggested we discuss our options, and that made sense. So I invited him over."

They went up the hall. Linda took her arm. "You're doing the right thing to keep your sense of humor. But I'm curious, is this positive attitude your doing or Robert's?"

Christina sighed. "The man does have a way about him."

"Given the evidence, who can argue with that?"

CHRISTINA HAD GOTTEN fresh flowers at the supermarket and she'd put on her best blouse, the cream satin one with narrow little pleats in front. She wore it with a dark green velvet skirt. It wasn't tight. She looked trim as ever. Joyce had said it would be a while before she began noticing a change in her weight.

It seemed odd that she cared about impressing Robert, but in a way, this was like their first date. Lunch didn't count since it was supposedly a business meeting, even though they'd hardly discussed business at all.

Christina had joked about it with Linda, but the truth was, she wasn't at all sure how she felt about Robert—either what was happening between them or what she wanted to happen. True, it felt good to have someone in the boat with her. She hadn't been exaggerating when she told Linda that. But Robert's pony remark had been weighing on her. Not to mention the fact that he'd embraced the notion of being a father pretty damned quick. Maybe too quick.

She'd been reluctant to press him about his expectations because it was safer to let things drift. That might have been a mistake. There were a hundred potential pitfalls. What if their expectations were incompatible? She didn't know whether to worry or not. Was she borrowing trouble? Or being a naive fool?

Of course, it wasn't necessarily a bad thing if Robert ended up playing an active role in the baby's life. If he were a good father it could prove to be a positive factor—not only for the baby, but for her, as well. She'd been pretty quick herself to say that her child was her responsibility, and hers alone.

If anything was clear to her, it was that there were a lot more questions than answers. And not surprisingly, most of them turned on Robert Williams.

She was in the kitchen, checking the baked potatoes, when the downstairs buzzer sounded. She went to the intercom by the front door.

"Robert?"

"Yep, it's me," came the increasingly familiar voice over the speaker.

"Come on up." She buzzed him in.

Christina took off her apron and carried it to the kitchen. Then she checked her face in the bathroom mirror. She seemed a bit flushed, but that was a symptom of pregnancy, too. Looking at herself, she realized she was beginning to think of herself as pregnant. She hoped that was a good sign.

Robert rapped on the door and she opened it. He stood there, his arms full of beautiful packages and an enormous bouquet of red roses. Half a dozen balloons floated over his head.

"It's a little early, I know," he said as she stared at him, "but happy Mother's Day."

"Robert..."

"Hey, we've already established that I'm a romantic, so I have nothing to lose by milking this for all it's worth." Giving her a wink, he stepped in without waiting to be invited, pausing only to kiss her on the cheek. "You're looking radiant tonight. Or am I projecting?" He dumped most of his goodies onto the sofa, then handed her the flowers and the balloons.

"Oh, my goodness," she said, looking at the balloons. One said, It's a Girl! Another, It's a Boy! There was a red one that said Mom. A large silver one had Congratulations!

Flustered, she sniffed the roses to hide her embarrassment. Her cheeks were undoubtedly as red as the flowers. "I've never seen so many roses in one bouquet."

"Two dozen," he said. "Twelve for you, twelve for the baby. Or twenty-three for you and one for the baby. I guess we should keep things in proportion. Don't want to spoil the kid before he or she gets here." He smiled. "By the way, when do we find out which we're having?"

"Can't you wait until it's born?"

"I thought everyone found out in advance these days."

She chuckled. "I don't think it's mandatory, Robert."

He fell silent, studying her. His initial effusiveness had given way to a more contemplative frame of mind. Was he savoring her, or savoring his fantasy?

"What are you thinking?" she asked, when he showed no sign of speaking.

"I don't know. How much I like this, I guess."

Christina wanted to feel that way herself, but something held her back. Fear, probably. This wasn't just fun and games. This was real life. The consequences stage. "I'd better go put these in water," she said. "Make yourself at home."

She went off to tend to the flowers. His positive attitude was refreshing—and it did tend to lift her spirits—but she couldn't help reminding herself that it was not very realistic. Someone had to look at this thing for what it was—a mistake that led to an unwanted pregnancy.

She laid the roses on the kitchen counter and got a vase down from an upper shelf in the cupboard.

"You've got a nice place here," he called out from the front room.

"Thanks. It's modest, but it serves my purposes."

Robert came to the kitchen door and stepped in. "How many bedrooms?"

"Just one."

"What about the baby? Where are you going to put him?"

"I haven't gotten to that point yet."

"We've obviously got some planning to do," he said.

"*We?*"

"Don't fathers get a vote?"

"On *my* living arrangements? Hardly." Again, his audacity surprised her, though she ought to be getting used to it by now. "Surely you're joking."

"No, I'm dead serious. We're in this together . . . for the long haul."

"Robert," she said, shaking her head, "you can't waltz in here with some balloons and presents and expect me to fall all over myself letting you change my life."

"It's not just your life, Christina. It's our life, and it's our baby."

She put her hands on her hips and glared at him. "God help my son if he turns out to be as arrogant as his father!"

Robert laughed. "And God help all the little boys if my daughter turns out to be as beautiful as her mother."

Taking her chin, he leaned forward and kissed her sweetly on the lips. "By the way, what's for dinner? Anything I can do to help?"

15

CHRISTINA PUT DOWN her fork and leaned back, looking past the single flickering candle at Robert. He seemed as contented as she.

"It was a great dinner," he said. "Fabulous, in fact."

She chuckled. "Don't you think you might be idealizing it just a bit? It was only a steak."

"But it was a great steak."

"Thanks, but that's not my point. What I'm trying to say is, you're romanticizing everything. Me, the dinner...especially the fact that I'm pregnant. You hear the word *baby* and you think it's some sort of mystical proof we're going to wind up together. You have visions of a white picket fence around a vine-covered bungalow, a floppy dog on the front lawn and eternal bliss."

"More like a stucco ranch house, some quarter horses out in the pasture and eternal bliss."

She rolled her eyes. "Now you're making fun of me."

"No," he said. "I'm only pointing out that the details are unimportant. From my perspective, it's you who matters. Everything that's happened between us was meant to be. I can feel it."

He peered across the table, smiling, the look of a prophet in his eyes. He was so damned sure of himself. Why couldn't she believe in fate that way? Probably because she'd never believed in fairy tales. In fact, she was a dyed-in-the-wool pragmatist.

Bill hadn't so much wooed her as she had convinced herself that marrying him was wise. And God knew, charm had never particularly impressed her before. Yet for some reason Robert's brand of charm was doing strange things to her. Christina had to summon every bit of her willpower to keep herself from swallowing his dream, hook, line and sinker.

"I'll clear the table," she said, getting up. "You go make yourself comfortable and I'll join you in a minute."

Robert got up, too. "No, you cooked. Now it's your turn to relax. I'll do it."

She started to protest, but he insisted, shooing her away. Christina went to the loveseat, liking it that he wanted to clean up for her. Bill would never have done that. Of course, for all she knew, under normal circumstances, Robert wouldn't be doing it either. He was obviously trying to make an impression.

She picked up one of the yellow sleepers he'd brought for the baby. The sight of the tiny dangling feet put a lump in her throat the size of an apple. There were other gifts, as well. A hooded bathing towel, two pairs of overalls and a little jacket with a ball and bat and the name Mariners on the front and a number 1 on the back. He'd also brought a soft teddy bear, a stuffed lamb, teething rings and rattles.

"If my mother were still living, she'd kill you," Christina had told him when she'd first opened the gifts.

"For stealing her thunder?"

"Exactly."

Robert had also given her a copy of one of his books and a complete set of the videocassettes of his TV series. "Might as well see how I spend my time," he'd explained.

She caressed the tiny sleeper, imagining her baby in it—a plump little body with arms and legs waving. To think, in only a few months there'd be a tiny person wearing these clothes, a baby that was half her and half Robert.

Just then Robert joined her on the loveseat. "I finished rinsing everything," he said.

"Thanks."

He looked down at the yellow sleeper lying on her knee and took the tiny foot in his hand, playing with it.

"Kind of puts you in awe of nature, doesn't it?" he said.

"Yes," she said, unconsciously touching her stomach, "it does. In fact, I've been sitting here with a lump in my throat just thinking about it."

Robert lightly ran his index finger over the back of her hand. When she turned and looked into his eyes, he kissed her. Christina kissed him back. Visions of Hawaii came to mind—the moonlight outside his bungalow, her ravenous desire for him. Their kiss became more intense.

Finally, she pulled her mouth free and looked away. "See how easily I get seduced by your game," she said. "You'd think I'd learn, wouldn't you?"

He rubbed her lower lip with his thumb. "If you like the ride, why not let go and enjoy it?"

"The ride isn't the issue, it's the results."

"Ah, yes. The pragmatist speaks. Well then," Robert said, "since you're so pragmatic, we should talk about some practical things. I believe that's why you invited me over."

She nodded.

"Well, from my standpoint, I have to decide what I'll be doing the next eight months."

Christina looked at him out of the corner of her eye. "I'm sure you have a plan."

"Yes, I've been thinking about getting a place in Seattle. I can write anywhere . . . so why not here, near . . ."

"The baby?"

"And you."

She could tell by the timbre of his voice it was his way of saying he wanted to be involved in her life. The problem was, she wasn't sure how she felt about that. Even though she'd known it was coming, even though she'd tried to prepare herself for it, Robert's comment took her by surprise.

"You want to watch my stomach grow, is that it?"

"Yeah, that's exactly it." Robert ran his finger across the side of her neck, making her shiver. "Hell, we've already made a baby. Why not have a relationship?"

She closed her eyes and took a deep breath, collecting herself. "A part of me wants to say yeah, that's a great idea. I mean, I don't like the idea of facing parenthood alone. But that's not a very good reason and, to be frank, where you're concerned, I don't trust my feelings."

"You're saying you don't believe in love at first sight."

"No. I believe in instant attraction, of course. But that's different."

"Whether you're ready to admit it or not, this thing between us is more than that. You're still hung up on the idea that I was the guy in the wrong bed. But you can't hide behind those Mai Tais and the Maui moon forever. You've got to come to terms with the fact that I'm the father of your child. You've got to give me a chance."

"Tell me something. Was your marriage a fairy tale? When you met your wife was it love at first sight?"

"No. Laura and I had known each other all through college. We were friends first. In time we came to love each other. And that's why we married."

"Were you happy?"

"We had our problems, of course. But we had a good marriage and we were looking forward to having a family."

Christina heard a tremor in his voice. "Have you considered that your feelings for me—your reaction to me being pregnant—might be because you lost your wife when she was expecting?"

"I don't regard you as a substitute, Christina. If that's what you're worried about, you can put it out of your mind."

"How can you be sure?"

"Because this a totally different feeling. I feel passion for you I've never felt for anyone else, even Laura. But you're right. It's all happened very fast. I'm a romantic, yes. But I'm also a skeptic. That's why I want to spend time with you, get to know you and have you know me."

Christina got up and went over to her front window, the sleeper still in her hand. She clutched it to her stomach and looked out into the darkness. The wind had come up. She could hear it whistling outside her window. She shivered.

Robert got up and came over, standing behind her. She could see his reflection in the glass.

"What do you want me to do?" he said softly. "How can I make it easier for you?"

"I'm tempted to say go on back to Santa Fe and when the baby's born, come back and we'll talk about it. But I know that's running from the problem."

He took her by the shoulders and turned her around. He lifted her chin to make her look at him. "Is that what you really want? Would you feel better if I went away?"

"I need time to think. But . . ."

"But what?"

"But I admit I don't like the idea of facing this by myself. And I do like you, Robert. I feel good when I'm with you, even if a part of me is really afraid."

He folded her into his arms, holding her. She hugged him back. Within moments she was crying. Robert stroked her head.

"Why do I do this?" she said, sniffling. "One minute I'm talking about sending you away, the next I want you to hold me and never let me go. It's as bad as that last night at the Coral Reef. First I told you to leave. A few seconds later I let you carry me off to bed."

"We've already agreed I'm irresistible."

She gave him a pinch. "And I'm gullible."

He tenderly kissed her mouth, running his hands up and down her back. "Are you feeling gullible now?" he whispered into her hair.

She started feeling desire again—the same desire that had been her undoing on Maui. "You're a bastard, Mr. Williams, you truly are," she said, kissing his chin.

"If I stay the night, we don't have to make love," he told her.

She chuckled. "'Come into my parlor,' said the spider to the fly."

He gave her a quirky smile. "So tell me, Christina, how do you feel about spiders?"

"I've never known one I could trust," she said, lifting her brow.

HE LAY ON HER BED in the white terry robe that he'd accepted with the utmost reluctance. "I bought it," she'd explained, "and Bill hasn't worn it all that often, so it's more mine than his. Anyway, it's been washed. And if you're going to stay, you might as well be comfortable."

He hadn't liked the idea, but he'd relented. After she'd gone off to the bath, he'd stripped and put on the robe. Then he'd gotten the candle from the dining table to make the mood more romantic.

He lay on the bed, watching the shadows flickering on the ceiling, contemplating her left-handed invitation to spend the night. Finally the door opened and she appeared, wearing a white terry robe of her own. For several moments she stood looking at him. He was on the sheets, the covers folded back at his feet.

"I was afraid you'd fallen asleep in there," he said.

"I've been working up my courage."

She smiled self-consciously. He could tell she was nervous. Somehow he found that endearing.

"I don't know why, but I'm trembling," she said. "I feel like this is the first time I've ever been with you."

"Then come over here and let me try to refresh your memory." He extended his hand and she crawled next to him. Robert rolled to his side, propping himself up with his elbow. He touched her cheek with the backs of his fingers, marveling at how far they'd come in only a few short weeks. He wanted her as he did before—passionately, completely—but his desire was more quiet now. He felt protective of her, wanting to give her happiness as well as pleasure.

"So here we are, no Mai Tais, no tropical air," he said. "Just you. Just me."

"You're forgetting someone, aren't you?"

The corner of his mouth curled. "And Junior makes three."

Her brow furrowed. Robert scooted closer, leaned over and kissed her.

"That second night in Hawaii you were fighting your desire," he whispered. "All that's stopping you now is your fear."

"Fear can be overwhelming," she murmured.

"Don't be afraid, Christina."

He rolled onto his back and took her hand, interlacing his fingers in hers. They lay like that for several moments. Robert watched the shadows flickering on the ceiling, very aware of her beside him. It was all he could do to keep from taking her into his arms and squeezing her with all his might.

It wasn't a sexual thing. He just wanted to possess her the way a person wanted to possess any treasured thing. And protect her—that instinct was very strong. He restrained himself, though. She needed quiet affection and he was determined to give it to her.

She rubbed her foot against his ankle. "You're warm," she said.

"You're cold."

"I know," she said, "I hate winter. I can never get warm at night."

"You need a man, Christina."

She rolled onto her side, facing him. "Funny you should say that. My mother used to preach that all the time. 'Christina,' she'd say, 'resign yourself to the fact that, women's liberation or not, no woman can survive without either an electric blanket or a man. Not in the winter, anyway.'"

"Smart lady, your mother."

"I'm sorry you'll never get to meet her."

"Well, I know her daughter, and that right there tells me a lot about her. She must have been a very special lady."

Christina's eyes instantly teared up. It must have been the right thing to say. He smiled and so did she.

"That's a very nice sentiment," she said.

"And heartfelt."

She reached over and fiddled with the lapels of his robe. It was an innocent gesture but an intimate one. He stared at her scrubbed face, her flawless features, the love welling inside him.

"Robert, if you were to stay Seattle, what would you expect?"

He shrugged. "Just that we be together."

"You mean like this?"

She drew her finger through the chest hair at the opening of his robe. He felt his heart lope. "If this was what you wanted."

"I don't necessarily mean being in bed together," she said. "I was thinking of dinner together, spending a quiet evening."

She pressed her palm against his chest and rubbed lightly, sliding her fingers under the edge of the robe. "Sure," he said, swallowing, "I'm all for quiet evenings."

"Sex doesn't necessarily follow friendship," she said as she caressed his chest.

"No . . . you could . . . argue that, I guess."

Christina ran her foot up and down the side of his calf. He felt himself grow hard.

"But it might be difficult to be around each other and not get the wrong idea," she said.

"Well, that's a point," he said, clearing his throat.

"Like even right now I'm tempted to run my hand right down your robe," she went on. "Despite everything I've said."

He drew a deep breath. "Are you trying to torture me, Christina?"

"No," she replied, "but I think I want to make love with you."

Robert took her hand and drew it to his lips, kissing it. "But will you hate me in the morning? That's the question."

"No. Maybe myself, but not you."

"I don't want you to hate yourself either. That's sort of what happened at the Coral Reef. And personally, I'm trying to take a long-range view."

She moved over him so that her face was above his. She kissed his mouth. "I might as well face the truth. I'm probably every bit as much of a romantic as you. I'm just not so quick to admit it."

He kissed her deeply and she responded as she did in Hawaii, her excitement and desire matching his. Within moments they were caught up in their lovemaking. It was less frenetic than it had been at the Coral Reef, but there was a warmth and an intimacy that was even better. He knew this woman, whereas that goddess had been a stranger.

"Christina, I love you," he whispered as he kissed her neck and shoulders. "I love you so much."

"Oh . . . Robert . . ." she murmured. It was almost a sob.

They kissed again, and when she opened her legs, he moved between them, entering her carefully. She writhed under him, her breath coming in anxious gasps. Their bodies undulated together. He had to concentrate to keep from coming, but he held back until he knew she was ready.

They came together, Christina digging her fingers into his back, lifting herself hard against him, gasping for breath. She lay there in the thrall of her pleasure. He felt the pulsing of her body slowly subside.

"Oh, Robert," she moaned again.

He held her, kissing her skin, cherishing her. She groaned and sank to his chest as her orgasm subsided. He was unable to move. Christina stayed where she was, with him still inside her. After a long, gauzy moment, he realized she was asleep. He moved to her side.

He reached down and carefully covered her with the blanket. Then he snuggled as close to her as he could, putting his arm around her waist.

Robert was tired, but he didn't think he'd sleep right away. Instead he lay there, thinking that the luckiest moment of his life was when he went into that travel agency and got the tickets for Maui. Finding Christina in Hawaii hadn't only changed his life, it had created a new life. How lucky could one man be?

16

As Christina made coffee the next morning, her mind was on Robert and all the wonderful things that had happened the night before. She decided that maybe this wasn't a fluke. Maybe this was the real thing—and not just because of the way he made her feel when they made love.

"Is that coffee I smell?" he said, appearing at the kitchen door. Robert was in the white terry robe, like her, his hair wet from his shower.

"It'll be ready in a few minutes. How about some scrambled eggs and toast to go with it?"

"Sounds good."

Robert came over and put his arms around her, hugging her from behind as she stood at the counter. He kissed her neck, sparking recollections of the night before.

"Mmm," she said, drawing her hand along the side of his face, "you've got a magic touch, don't you?"

"You inspire me."

"Is it me?"

"What else?" He gave her a firm squeeze, holding her abdomen in his large warm hands as he kissed her neck again. "I'm pretty fond of Junior, too."

"Maybe it's Junior you're enamored with, not me."

"No, that's just the frosting on the cake."

"How do I know that?" she asked.

"I knew you first."

"What if I wasn't pregnant? Would you still be here this morning?"

"Yep, but without the balloons."

That made her smile. She didn't want to think the baby made the critical difference. Their attraction certainly had nothing to do with it. Even so, she couldn't deny that the fact that she was pregnant did make a difference—at least with her. As the father of her child, she couldn't help but see Robert in a different light.

She pulled away from his arms and went to the fridge to get the eggs. Robert leaned against the counter, watching, as she cracked half a dozen eggs into a bowl.

"Ever been on a ranch?" he asked.

Christina looked at him. "No, not really. Driving by one is about as close as I've ever gotten."

"How'd you like to visit mine?"

"You want me to visit your ranch?" she said, adding a splash of milk to the eggs.

"Yeah."

"Why?"

"I've seen you in your element," he said. "It seems only fair that you see me in mine."

She set down the bowl and turned the burner on under the skillet. "What is it about men, anyway? Give 'em an inch and they want a mile."

"Maybe I should skip the preliminaries," he said, "and get right to my point. How do you feel about marriage?"

Christina was stunned. "Marriage?"

"Yeah, as in you and me."

It took her a moment to gather her thoughts. "I know you like to move at light speed, but isn't this a little quick—even for you?"

He shrugged. "What's the problem?"

Christina put some bread in the toaster, then turned to face him. "You're kidding, aren't you?"

"No, actually I'm not. The wedding doesn't have to be this weekend. There's no big rush."

"Well, that's a relief." She pointed to the plates and flatware she'd gotten out. "How'd you like to set the table?"

"Sure. I'll take the coffee in, too."

As Robert went off to the other room, Christina thought about what had just happened. He was serious about them getting married. But how could he be? If she'd learned anything about Robert Williams, it was that he wasn't a fool. To the contrary, he was an intelligent man. Yet he seemed so certain of the way he felt, that he was already talking marriage.

She dumped the eggs in the sizzling skillet and began to stir. Why couldn't she feel that kind of certainty? What was holding her back? She loved being with him, loved making love with him. Never before had she felt such passion for and with a man. Was that true love?

He returned to the kitchen. "Everything's ready. What now?"

"The eggs are just about done."

The toast popped up. Robert stepped over and tended to it while Christina finished cooking the eggs.

She took the pan off the burner and they both went to the table. Christina divided the eggs between their plates, then took the pan back to the kitchen, grabbing some jam from the fridge on her way back. Robert held her chair for her, then took his place.

"Hypothetical situation—" he tore off a piece of toast and smeared jam over it "—by way of continuing our conversation. Say we'd been living together a year. Would we have been equally considerate to one another about how we got breakfast on the table?"

"Probably not," she said, taking a sip of coffee.

He took a bite of eggs. "How bad would it have been?"

"You've halfway convinced me you're a nice guy, but I sense domesticity isn't the real you. I'd end up doing most of the cooking."

"Is that all right with you?"

She chuckled. "My mother once told me the secret to having a good marriage is not expecting too much of your husband."

"I'd have gotten along well with your mom."

The thought was actually sort of amusing. When Christina reflected on it, she decided her mother would have liked Robert Williams. *He's a charming man*, she could hear her mother say, *and so good-looking*.

"But the more important question," he said, "is how well you and I would get along."

"I can be pretty bitchy at times. You haven't seen that side of me yet."

Robert took another bite of eggs. "Well, I've got a temper, so I'm not perfect, either."

"Are you trying to discourage me?" She sipped her coffee, looking at him over the rim of her cup.

"Nope. I'm just trying to find out how much time you need before you'd consider marriage. I mean, we've already got a baby on the way. You've got to admit it would be convenient if the little tyke had a mother *and* a father around."

She put down her fork and looked him in the eye. "You might as well know right now, I'm not about to marry you just because I'm pregnant."

"No, and I wouldn't either if I were in your shoes. And that isn't why I'm asking, by the way."

Christina began eating again. "I'm not sure I can give you an answer to that. I think when the time comes, I'll just know. Maybe something'll happen that will make it all crystal clear."

There was an unexpected knock on the door. They looked toward it with surprise.

"Who could that be?" she mumbled.

The words were no sooner out of her mouth than they heard the sound of a key in the lock.

"Oh, my God," Christina said, her hands going to her mouth.

The door opened slightly.

"Chris!" came Bill's voice. "It's me. I caught an early flight." The door opened farther. "Are you here..." His voice faded as he saw them. His mouth dropped open.

"Bill," she said, jumping to her feet. She made her way to him, pulling her robe more tightly closed and cinching the belt. "I thought you were coming tonight. I didn't expect you."

Bill was dumbfounded, looking past her at Robert, the surprise on his face turning first to dismay, then anger. "No, I guess you weren't expecting me. What in the hell is he doing here? How long has this been going on?"

"I know you're shocked," she said, taking his arm.

He jerked his arm free, still glaring at Robert. "The bastard's even wearing my robe."

Christina glanced back at Robert, who'd gotten to his feet. She could tell trouble, serious trouble, was brewing. "If you'll just calm down, Bill, I'll explain."

"Calm down?" he roared. "I walk in on the woman I'm going to marry, find her half-undressed and with some jerk we ran into in Hawaii, and you tell me to calm down?"

"Bill," Robert said, "Christina is trying to explain, if you'll just give her a chance."

Bill pointed a threatening finger. "Listen, buddy, you stay out of this. This is between Christina and me."

"Then show a little respect."

Bill started across the room toward Robert, but she grabbed him. "Bill, if you want an explanation, I'll give it to you. But you can't act like a schoolboy."

"I'm not going to have that S.O.B. telling me what to do."

"Just calm down." She turned to Robert. "Please, let me handle this."

He folded his arms and Christina backed Bill into the nearest chair.

"I'm terribly sorry you had to find out this way," she said. "I'd planned to tell you tonight."

"Chris," he lamented, "surely you aren't having an affair with this guy."

She sighed woefully, glancing over at Robert. She could tell he was struggling to keep from grinning. She gave him an admonishing look and turned back to Bill.

"Something happened in Hawaii, something that started out as an innocent mistake, but turned into . . . well . . ."

"Turned into what?"

"Bill, the bottom line is I'm pregnant. I'm going to have Robert's baby."

Bill was in virtual shock. "What?"

"It's a long story, but you're entitled to hear it."

Bill slumped in his chair, dazed, as she proceeded to relate what had happened during those two days they'd spent at the Coral Reef. When she'd finished, he shook his head in utter disbelief.

"But why is he here now? Did he spend the night? Chris, I can't believe you'd do this with some guy who—"

"Listen, Bill," Robert said, moving toward them, "Christina has tried to spare your feelings. What happened in Hawaii wasn't planned. God knows neither of us intended that she get pregnant, nor did we intend to fall in love. I'm here because we care for each other and want to be together. You've been blindsided, I know, but this wasn't what Christina chose. You were gone when I arrived in Seattle, and this is the first chance she's had to tell you."

Bill looked up at her. "I can understand a mistake. I can understand that weird things happen. But you can't love this guy, Chris. We've been together for months.

You've been with him . . . what, a couple of days? How can you do this?"

Christina and Robert exchanged looks. Something in his eyes told her. It was like a veil of fog lifting. Suddenly she knew. Turning to Bill, she said, "I know it seems bizarre, but it's what I want. I love him, Bill. I truly love him."

"You're saying you've fallen for a virtual stranger?"

"I can't expect you to understand," she said. "I hardly understand myself. But one thing I'm sure of is I never felt this way before."

Bill looked back and forth between them, shaking his head. After a while he got to his feet and dragged himself to the door. Opening it, he looked back at her. "I'm counting on the fact that you'll come to your senses, Chris. When you do, give me a call." He left then, closing the door behind him.

She turned to Robert. He was contemplating her, a serious expression on his face. She drew a deep anguished breath.

"We seem to go from one unexpected turn to the next, don't we?" she lamented.

"It's fate, Christina."

"Do you think so?"

He nodded.

She moved to where he stood and he took her into his arms. He kissed her hair as they clung to each other.

"You know what appeals to me most?" he said.

"What?"

"That we're going to have the next fifty years to de-bate the point."

"Robert, if I'm foolish enough to marry you I'll end up—"

He put his finger to her lips, cutting her off. "You'll end up the happiest woman in the world."

"What makes you so sure?"

"I wouldn't have it any other way."

Epilogue

THE SUN SLOWLY SANK toward the horizon as Robert strolled along the beach. The warm, balmy air of Maui was a welcome change from the cold and snow in Santa Fe and the rain and wind in Seattle. There had been more snow at the ranch than usual for the holidays, so he especially appreciated the warm water of the Pacific lapping at his feet.

It was a year ago today that he'd arrived at the Coral Reef and taken a stroll along this same stretch of sand. How incredible those next few days had been. Even today he marveled at his good fortune. Before going on his stroll, he'd wandered through the garden and found the bench he'd been sitting on the first time he saw her. And though there'd been nobody standing by that column, he'd had no trouble picturing her there—long auburn hair blowing in the gentle breeze, classically beautiful. His goddess.

By the time he returned to the hotel, the sun had dropped from sight and the landscape was only faintly illuminated by the glow from the western sky. From the direction of the bungalows, huddled under the shadows of the palms, he saw her moving toward him, slender again, though still not quite as slender as before. But she hadn't lost the walk, or the elegant look. She was as appealing as ever—even more so, because his love for her, his appreciation of her, had continued to grow with each passing day.

She was in a green sarong that matched the emerald engagement ring he'd given her. Her hair fluttered lightly in the breeze. Her smile—which he could see now that she was closer—never ceased to take his breath away.

"Glad to see you found your way home," she said. "I was afraid you were washed out to sea or ran off with a mermaid or something."

Robert embraced her. "Now what would I do with a mermaid when I've already got the most beautiful creature on earth—land, air or sea?"

"The Maui air can do strange things to people," Christina said, "or have you forgotten?"

They started back toward the bungalow, their arms around each other's waist.

"I haven't forgotten. Nor am I taking any chances. I've advised the spa to escort every beautiful lady without a room key to bungalow 12."

"*Every* beautiful lady?"

"At least that way I'll be sure to get the right one. You can send the others away."

Christina laughed. "Maybe I'll send them over to bungalow 13. Maria would probably welcome the help."

"Was Jordan giving her a bad time?"

"He wasn't very happy until I went over to nurse him. But he calmed down. He was sleeping when I left. I just hope for her sake he sleeps through the night."

"What do you mean, for *her* sake?" he said. "Whenever you go jogging, you hear him crying a block away. That bungalow is just across the walk."

"But with the sound of the sea and the deep sleep you always seem to put me in, how will we hear him?"

"Christina, that kid has your lungs. I understand the staff here is still talking about that woman last year in bungalow 12."

She gave him a whack on the stomach. "What kind of husband are you to embarrass me that way?"

"Embarrass you? Darling, I couldn't be more proud."

"Of a wife who's vocal about her pleasure?"

"No," he said. "I'm proud that they're still talking about the guy who was with her."

Christina gave him a look. "Robert, you're terrible."

They'd reached the palms and stopped in the shadows. They turned and looked back at the last glow of light out over the sea.

"Beautiful, isn't it?" she said wistfully.

"I have lots of memories of this place, but none so wonderful as those two nights last year with you."

Christina kissed him and he held her close, savoring her scent, the feel of her body. He loved her with all his heart.

"Do you think it'll ever be that good again?" she asked.

"Of course. Even better. And now that you've recovered from giving birth there isn't any reason why I can't show you a wonderful time. That was half the reason I brought you here."

"Sounds like you've got it all worked out."

"I do."

"So, what are your plans for the evening?" she asked.

"Well, I thought we'd start with a nice romantic dinner, maybe with a few Mai Tais."

"No," Christina said. "No Mai Tais."

"Why not? You aren't pregnant anymore."

"Robert, the last drink I had was a year ago tonight. Look what happened!"

"Yeah, you've got a husband and a three-month-old son to show for it. What more could a woman ask for?"

"True, but I don't need a bunch of Mai Tais to enjoy either you or Jordan."

They leaned their heads together as they stared out at the falling dusk. Just then, behind them, they heard a baby's cry. Christina turned and looked toward bungalow 13, where their son was with his nanny.

"Oh, my," she said as the baby continued to cry.

"Maria will take care of him," Robert said. "Just relax."

They stood there for a moment or two longer and Jordan's cries got even more insistent. Robert could tell her maternal instinct had kicked in and she wasn't going to relax until the baby was quietly asleep.

"What do you think, Mom? You want to peek in and see what Jordan's problem is before I take you to dinner?"

"If you don't mind."

Christina kissed him on the cheek and started toward the bungalow. She stopped after a few steps.

"Robert?"

"Yes, darling?"

"Maybe I will let you buy me a few Mai Tais, after all."

He laughed. "I know, you're thinking maybe you'd like for Jordan to have a little sister."

Even in the dark he could see her roll her eyes. "Scratch the Mai Tais," she said dryly. "On second thought, I think I'll wait until next year."

Robert Williams laughed until tears came to his eyes. Mai Tais or not, they were going to have a wonderful night—he had a premonition. If it was possible for lightning to strike the same place twice, why not three times?

HARLEQUIN® *Temptation*

THE WRONG BED

The Wrong Bed? The Wrong Twin?
The Ultimate Temptation

It was ten years since Emily Rose had seen
"Chigger" Callister, but he'd grown up to be sheriff
of Bluster County and a magnificent specimen of
manhood, just as she'd pictured him in her bedtime
fantasies. She couldn't quite pin down his personality,
though. She never knew which Callister she was
going to see.

It was almost as if there were two of him.

Don't miss:

#591 TWIN BEDS
Regan Forest

Available in June wherever Harlequin books are sold.

Take 4 bestselling love stories FREE

Plus get a FREE surprise gift!

Special Limited-time Offer

Mail to Harlequin Reader Service®

3010 Walden Avenue
P.O. Box 1867
Buffalo, N.Y. 14269-1867

YES! Please send me 4 free Harlequin Temptation® novels and my free surprise gift. Then send me 4 brand-new novels every month, which I will receive before they appear in bookstores. Bill me at the low price of $2.66 each plus 25¢ delivery and applicable sales tax, if any.* That's the complete price and a savings of over 10% off the cover prices—quite a bargain! I understand that accepting the books and gift places me under no obligation ever to buy any books. I can always return a shipment and cancel at any time. Even if I never buy another book from Harlequin, the 4 free books and the surprise gift are mine to keep forever.

142 BPA AW6V

Name	(PLEASE PRINT)	
Address		Apt. No.
City	State	Zip

This offer is limited to one order per household and not valid to present Harlequin Temptation® subscribers. *Terms and prices are subject to change without notice. Sales tax applicable in N.Y.

UTEMP-995 ©1990 Harlequin Enterprises Limited

BRIDE'S BAY RESORT

UNLOCK THE DOOR TO GREAT ROMANCE AT BRIDE'S BAY RESORT

Join Harlequin's new across-the-lines series, set in an exclusive hotel on an island off the coast of South Carolina.

Seven of your favorite authors will bring you exciting stories about fascinating heroes and heroines discovering love at Bride's Bay Resort.

Look for these fabulous stories coming to a store near you beginning in January 1996.

Harlequin American Romance #613 in January
Matchmaking Baby by Cathy Gillen Thacker

Harlequin Presents #1794 in February
Indiscretions by Robyn Donald

Harlequin Intrigue #362 in March
Love and Lies by Dawn Stewardson

Harlequin Romance #3404 in April
Make Believe Engagement by Day Leclaire

Harlequin Temptation #588 in May
Stranger in the Night by Roseanne Williams

Harlequin Superromance #695 in June
Married to a Stranger by Connie Bennett

Harlequin Historicals #324 in July
Dulcie's Gift by Ruth Langan

Visit Bride's Bay Resort each month wherever Harlequin books are sold.

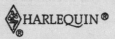

HARLEQUIN ®

Let this bestselling author introduce you to a
sizzling new page-turner!

She'll do anything.

Lie, cheat, steal—Caroline Hogarth will do anything
to get her little boy back. Her father-in-law will do
anything to prevent it. And there's no one in the city
he can't buy. Except, maybe, Jack Fletcher—a man
Caroline is prepared to seduce.

So what if he's a convicted murderer? So what if he's
a priest?

Watch the sparks fly this May.
Available wherever books are sold.

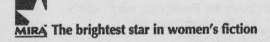 **The brightest star in women's fiction**

MJCNSTG

Bestselling authors

ELAINE COFFMAN
RUTH LANGAN
and
MARY McBRIDE

Together in one fabulous collection!

Available in June wherever Harlequin
books are sold.

HARLEQUIN®

Don't miss these Harlequin favorites by some of our most distinguished authors!
And now, you can receive a discount by ordering two or more titles!

HT #25645	THREE GROOMS AND A WIFE by JoAnn Ross	$3.25 U.S./$3.75 CAN.	☐
HT #25648	JESSIE'S LAWMAN by Kristine Rolofson	$3.25 U.S./$3.75 CAN.	☐
HP #11725	THE WRONG KIND OF WIFE by Roberta Leigh	$3.25 U.S./$3.75 CAN.	☐
HP #11755	TIGER EYES by Robyn Donald	$3.25 U.S./$3.75 CAN.	☐
HR #03362	THE BABY BUSINESS by Rebecca Winters	$2.99 U.S./$3.50 CAN.	☐
HR #03375	THE BABY CAPER by Emma Goldrick	$2.99 U.S./$3.50 CAN.	☐
HS #70638	THE SECRET YEARS by Margot Dalton	$3.75 U.S./$4.25 CAN.	☐
HS #70655	PEACEKEEPER by Marisa Carroll	$3.75 U.S./$4.25 CAN.	☐
HI #22280	MIDNIGHT RIDER by Laura Pender	$2.99 U.S./$3.50 CAN.	☐
HI #22235	BEAUTY VS THE BEAST by M.J. Rogers	$3.50 U.S./$3.99 CAN.	☐
HAR #16531	TEDDY BEAR HEIR by Elda Minger	$3.50 U.S./$3.99 CAN.	☐
HAR #16596	COUNTERFEIT HUSBAND by Linda Randall Wisdom	$3.50 U.S./$3.99 CAN.	☐
HH #28795	PIECES OF SKY by Marianne Willman	$3.99 U.S./$4.50 CAN.	☐
HH #28855	SWEET SURRENDER by Julie Tetel	$4.50 U.S./$4.99 CAN.	☐

(limited quantities available on certain titles)

	AMOUNT	$
DEDUCT:	**10% DISCOUNT FOR 2+ BOOKS**	$
ADD:	**POSTAGE & HANDLING**	$
	($1.00 for one book, 50¢ for each additional)	
	APPLICABLE TAXES**	$_____
	TOTAL PAYABLE	$_____
	(check or money order—please do not send cash)	

To order, complete this form and send it, along with a check or money order for the total above, payable to Harlequin Books, to: **In the U.S.:** 3010 Walden Avenue, P.O. Box 9047, Buffalo, NY 14269-9047; **In Canada:** P.O. Box 613, Fort Erie, Ontario, L2A 5X3.

Name: _____

Address: _____ City: _____

State/Prov.: _____ Zip/Postal Code: _____

**New York residents remit applicable sales taxes.
  Canadian residents remit applicable GST and provincial taxes.

HBACK-AJ3

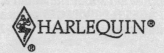

You're About to Become a *Privileged Woman*

Reap the rewards of fabulous free gifts and benefits with proofs-of-purchase from Harlequin and Silhouette books

Pages & Privileges™

It's our way of thanking you for buying our books at your favorite retail stores.

PROOF OF PURCHASE
HT-PP137
Offer expires October 31, 1996

**Harlequin and Silhouette—
the most privileged readers in the world!**

For more information about Harlequin and Silhouette's PAGES & PRIVILEGES program call the Pages & Privileges Benefits Desk: 1-503-794-2499

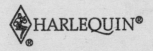

HARLEQUIN®

HT-PP137